"Who Said Anything About Getting Involved?"

Tom murmured. "I want you. You want me." He flashed her a roguish grin that made her heart skip a beat. "It would be the perfect arrangement."

His words had struck a raw spot. Tannis had lived without love in her life since she'd walked away from her marriage with her ego in shreds. To love would require that she trust again, that she give her heart. And she didn't think she could survive having her dreams crushed a second time.

She suddenly recognized how very vulnerable she was. Wrenching herself away from him, she took several rapid steps across the room before she turned to face him. "No, Tom. It wouldn't be perfect. Not for me."

Dear Reader,

Just when you thought Mother Nature had turned up the heat, along comes Silhouette Desire to make things even *hotter*. It's June...the days are longer, the kids are out of school, and we've got the very best that romance has to offer.

Let's start with our *Man of the Month, Haven's Call,* which is by Robin Elliott, a writer many of you have written to tell me is one of your favorites.

Next, we have *Salty and Felicia* by Lass Small. If you've ever wondered how those two older Browns got together, well, now you'll get to find out! From Jennifer Greene comes the latest installment in her JOCK'S BOYS series, *Bewildered*. And Suzanne Simms's series, HAZARDS, INC., continues with *The Pirate Princess*.

Anne Marie Winston has created a tender, wonderful story, *Substitute Wife*. And if you like drama and intensity with your romance, don't miss Lucy Gordon's *Uncaged!*

It just doesn't get any better than this...so read and enjoy.

All the best,

Lucia Macro
Senior Editor

Please address questions and book requests to:
Reader Service
U.S.: P.O. Box 1325, Buffalo, NY 14269
Canadian: P.O. Box 1050, Niagara Falls, Ont. L2E 7G7

ANNE MARIE WINSTON
SUBSTITUTE WIFE

SILHOUETTE *Desire*®
Published by Silhouette Books
America's Publisher of Contemporary Romance

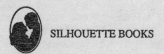 SILHOUETTE BOOKS

ISBN 0-373-05863-2

SUBSTITUTE WIFE

Copyright © 1994 by Anne Marie Rodgers

Printed in U.S.A.

ANNE MARIE WINSTON

A native Pennsylvanian and former educator, Anne Marie is a book lover, an animal lover and always a teacher at heart. She and her husband have two daughters and a menagerie of four-footed family members. When she's not parenting, writing or reading, she devotes her time to a variety of educational efforts in her community. Readers can write to Anne Marie at P.O. Box 302, Zullinger, PA 17272.

For Paula Pearl,
who gave me that first joyous chance.
And for Karen Taylor Richman,
whose constant encouragement, guidance and
championing of my career have meant more than mere
words can express.

One

Tannis Carlson slid open the glass door of her basement rec room and stepped out onto the concrete apron. Brrr! Forty degrees might be warm for a January evening in Virginia, but it was definitely the wrong weather for a woman to sashay around outside in nothing but a beach towel and bare skin. Too bad the people from whom she'd bought this house seven years ago hadn't built the hot tub in the basement.

Tannis scampered across the small space that separated her from the hot tub. A quick glance at the houses on either side assured her that no one was visible as she flipped back the tub's cover, releasing clouds of steam, which rose into the chilly night air. The trees at the back of the yard provided privacy from behind and a high wooden fence enclosed her little patio, shielding her from the neighbors' view ...

neighbor. Tom—*no!* Don't think of him. Not now, not ever.

She dropped the towel on a patio chair and quickly mounted the wooden steps to the tub. For a moment she lingered there, testing the temperature with her toe, then she slipped slowly into the heated water.

Ooh, it felt too hot. She stood and hauled herself up on the edge to check the temperature gauge. One hundred and three degrees. No, it wasn't too hot. She forced herself to sit again, disregarding the switches that would light the interior of the tub and make the water bubble around her. She liked sitting out here in the dark, dreaming. Now the water was...

Perfect. She sighed aloud and slid down a little farther on the bench seat, feeling the strains of the school day ease a bit with each minute that passed. But her other worries wouldn't be dismissed so easily. If only she could figure out a way to earn enough money to keep this house and still pay for her mother's care. If only the nursing home into which her mother had been moved wasn't so costly. If only teachers were better paid.

Time to face it, Tannis Anne, she told herself. *You're going to have to get a second job.* It was an unappetizing thought. Teaching a classroom full of fourth-graders was wearing, although she loved it. The mere idea of taking on a second job, an evening job, was almost too much to face. And what other kind of job could she get, anyway? She had no marketable skills other than her teaching expertise. Tutoring was a possibility, but that was sort of seasonal.

She supposed she could apply at some of the local stores—perhaps she could work as a clerk in the evenings and on weekends. Or maybe a bank would take her on as a teller—

"I bet the water feels great tonight."

Tannis jumped and nearly screamed, biting back the sound at the last moment as she recognized the deep, smooth voice of her neighbor, Tom Hayes. It wasn't a conscious recognition, she knew. Her body would recognize Tom Hayes anytime, anywhere. Her heart picked up its pace, but she firmly ignored the insistent flutter beneath her breastbone.

"Tom, you rat. You scared me out of three years' growth." She was breathless from more than fright and she hoped he didn't know it. "What are you doing sneaking around out here?" She fought to keep the jittery nerves out of her voice as she slid down a little farther beneath the surface. She felt horribly exposed but surely he couldn't see her in the dark, could he? Why, oh, why hadn't she turned on those blasted jets?

"I wanted to talk to you," said her neighbor, not bothering to defend himself. "I called, but you didn't answer. I saw your car and I thought you were home. Amy said you often hop in the hot tub at night, so I figured I'd come on over for a minute."

"Are the kids in bed?" Tannis narrowed her eyes so she could see Tom through the steam swirling from the surface of the tub. He stood with a foot cocked on one of the steps that led up to the pool, one elbow resting on his denim-clad knee. A heavy down jacket hung from his broad shoulders, and the flannel shirt beneath was open at the neck, showing a wealth of dark curls at his throat. As usual, the mere sight of him provoked a heated reaction in the pit of her stomach.

Quit panting, Tannis Anne. He's not for you.

No, he definitely wasn't the man for her. Still, the memory of a heated kiss on a darkened doorstep stirred. Ruthlessly she shoved it away. That kiss had been a mistake, one she'd regretted for nearly four years.

But her reaction to Tom Hayes had been out of her control since the first time she'd met him nearly eight years ago, when he was her friend Mary's husband. She could still remember how shocked she'd been when he'd shaken her hand and she'd felt the sizzle between them so strongly that her toes had curled inside her shoes. What was it about him, she wondered, that overloaded her circuits?

Her neighbor wasn't handsome, by any stretch of the imagination. His craggy features were as roughly hewn as the ancient mountains that rose to the northwest, but his compelling aura of sexuality had drawn Tannis like a magnet since the first time she'd met him. The only truly beautiful thing about him was his eyes, an unusual silvery green that deepened to emerald when he was angry and glittered like the sunlit sea when he was amused. On the few occasions when Tom had relaxed enough to smile, his blunt features rearranged themselves into a breathtaking mixture of masculine charm and little-boy appeal that no woman could hope to resist.

Lucky for her Tom didn't smile much. Losing his wife, Mary, to cancer three years ago had taken away most of Tom's rare smiles for good. If only his sex appeal had gone, as well.

"Yeah, Jeb and Amy are in bed."

His answer scattered her thoughts and forced her to remember what the conversation had been about.

When Tom didn't add anything further, she prodded. "You said you wanted to talk to me?"

"Jebbie said you didn't have enough money to get your car fixed." Tom's words were a shock. His silvery eyes pierced through the mist around Tannis and made her feel as though he could see every thought in her head.

"Jebbie talks too much," Tannis muttered, mentally vowing to be more careful about her words in front of Tom's six-year-old son. Then she rallied. "My finances are none of your business. But you can tell Jebbie I got my car straightened out. The distributor cap was cracked."

"Why did you tell Jeb you didn't have the money to fix it?"

She sighed. Tom wouldn't be deterred once he was on the trail of something. "I didn't. He listened in on one of my telephone conversations. Besides, I found the money to fix it. Why did you come over here?"

"To talk to you about a job offer."

He couldn't have surprised her more if he'd announced he was planning to move to the Caribbean. Since Mary's death, Tom had backed away from her offers of help. He'd withdrawn from the comfort and the need to share the death of someone they'd both loved, and Tannis hadn't been able to breach his silence. Finally she'd given up trying, contenting herself with being a friend to Mary's children.

Mary. She could still recall the last promise she'd made to her dying friend as she sat near her bed one of the last days of Mary's life.

"Tannis...will you promise me something?" Mary's voice was thin and thready. The pain had become intense in the past few days and most of her remaining energy was expended fighting it off.

"You know I'll do anything I can for you." Tannis leaned close to the bed and gently clasped Mary's hand in hers. "What is it?"

"Help Tom take care of Amy and Jebbie. He's . . . going to need you."

Tannis had promised through the lump that clogged her throat. Mary had been understanding and kind, the dearest friend she'd ever had, and she'd deserved more loyalty from Tannis than she'd gotten. Oh, what she wouldn't have given to erase that kiss from her past!

A bare week later, Mary had lost her battle with the cancer.

But Tom hadn't allowed her to help or support him. He'd shut her out with a finality that had hurt and saddened her.

"Don't you want to hear what I'm offering?" His voice interrupted the flash of memory.

Cautiously she said, "I already have a job, Tom. Are you proposing I give up teaching?"

"No. I was thinking of something that wouldn't interfere with your job."

"Such as?"

Tom didn't answer directly. "Mrs. Cutter resigned today, effective the end of the month."

Tannis knew Mrs. Cutter was the baby-sitter who'd kept Tom's children before and after school since Mary's death. Now she had an inkling of what he wanted, but she only said, "That's too bad. I know the kids like her."

"Yeah." Tom shifted his weight to the other hip.

The motion brought him closer to the edge of the hot tub and Tannis instantly slid a bit farther down on the seat. Mary had been a slim, svelte brunette, not a short, chubby redhead, and Tannis had no intention of letting Tom compare her all-too-generous measurements with those of his late, lovely wife's.

"I was wondering if you'd consider taking care of the kids," Tom said. His voice was slow and deep as he went on. "They love you. I'd pay you the same thing I pay Mrs. Cutter. It amounts to about three hours a day."

She knew his hours were dependable. Tom was a lawyer. He often said he handled the dull stuff—wills and estates—although Tannis had never thought anything about Tom Hayes could be labeled "dull." Still, she knew he could be counted on to be home by five each night.

Aloud, she said, "I'll have to think about it, Tom."

"What is there to think about? You know my kids. They could come to your classroom at the end of the day and ride home with you."

"You don't think Amy's too old for a baby-sitter? Why couldn't she watch Jeb after school? She's twelve, Tom. A lot of girls begin baby-sitting for others at that age."

Tom hesitated. "I wouldn't feel comfortable knowing the kids were unsupervised for an hour and a half every morning and afternoon. Amy likes you. I don't think she'd pitch a fit about coming home with you."

Tannis arched her brows. She couldn't imagine cheerful, bouncy Amy pitching a fit over anything. She nodded. "It would be a good solution to your problem, and I'd like to consider the idea. But I need some time to think about it."

Tom grunted. He'd clearly expected her to capitulate without an argument. "Will Saturday be enough time?"

She shrugged, and instantly cursed herself as the water danced vigorously around her bare shoulders. "I suppose."

"Good." Tom shifted back away from the hot tub and she suppressed a sigh of relief. "Why don't you come over for dinner? The kids have been bugging me to ask you over, and we can talk after they go to bed."

"That would be fine. What can I bring?" She deliberately kept her voice cool and unenthusiastic.

"Don't worry about bringing anything," Tom said, stepping back another pace, scattering her thoughts. "I'll handle the meal. Just come over around five."

He turned and departed, and his leaving reminded her vividly of a night four years ago, shortly after Mary had gotten ill.

They had had a fight earlier in the week, Tom and Mary. Jebbie was less than two years old and Amy was in second grade. She didn't know exactly what had been the trouble between them, but she remembered Mary asking her to baby-sit on a Saturday night.

"We need some time to talk without kids," she'd said soberly.

So Tannis had kept baby Jeb and Amy while they'd gone out to dinner and a movie. Jeb had been teething and she'd walked circles around their house with the fussy toddler. Toward eleven, his fussiness escalated into full-scale screaming and when Tom and Mary came home, Mary gave her a fleeting grin before whisking him off to the upstairs nursery. "The only thing that helps when he gets like this is Mom," she'd said.

Tannis had protested when Tom walked her to her door—she only lived a few yards away. But he'd been adamant.

On her small, enclosed porch, he'd appeared to want to linger.

"So how was dinner?" she asked.

Tom shrugged. "Not so good, if you want to know the truth."

Tannis was silent. She didn't really want to hear about Tom and Mary's problems but he seemed to need to talk.

"We have…a big difference of opinion on how she should proceed with her treatment." Tom turned away from her and stuffed his hands into his pants pockets. His broad shoulders were tense and set and she heard the deep breath he drew in hitch at the end. "God, I'm so afraid. What will I do without her? If she dies—"

"Shhh." Acting on impulse, needing to comfort him, she slipped to his side and wrapped an arm around his hard, lean middle, placing her other hand over his lips. "Don't borrow trouble. Not yet. Surely the doctor will talk to her…" Her words trailed away.

Tom had raised his hands to her shoulders. Slowly he reached up and drew her hand away, placing it on his shoulder. "Tannis. I need you." His hands tightened on her shoulders as he drew her to him.

Her pulse skipped a beat then doubled its pace, but she told herself he only needed comfort. Comfort. She could offer him that. She allowed him to embrace her as she circled his neck with both arms. "I know, Tom. I know—"

Then his lips came down on hers.

A surge of heat raced through her. It was like touching an electric fence, only there was no pain. She tried to pull back but his grip on her shoulders was firm. His face was close and his lips slid onto hers again, rocking the foundations of her world. How could this feel so right when she knew it was wrong? Or was it wrong? How could it be wrong if it felt so right? She didn't protest, couldn't, as he kissed her, gently increasing the sweet pressure of his mouth until his tongue was probing delicately at the closed line of her lips.

Her hands clenched in his hair. She opened her mouth.

Tom groaned deep in his throat. His tongue surged forward in a blatant mating quest as his hands slid down her back and pressed her body against every hard inch of his.

How long did it last, that wild, hot, ravenous kissing? She never knew. Not long enough. Too long.

Long enough for a trickle of guilt to finally become a roaring deluge in her head. *This was her best friend's husband!*

She wanted to accede to every exciting demand he was making on her, but a shred of sanity tore her mouth from beneath his.

"What are we doing, Tom?"

It was a ragged gasp of sound, but it got through to him. His hands stilled on her body, though he didn't release her.

Again, she tried. "Tom, I find you very attractive. But we both care for Mary. This would hurt her terribly."

"You're right." He lowered his forehead to hers. "I don't know what got into me."

"Moonlight madness," she offered. "Comfort that got out of hand. Now let me go in and we'll both forget this ever happened."

He nodded, but still he didn't move away. Finally she pressed her hands to his shoulders lightly. He released her and stepped back, exhaling a deep, mournful sigh. "Ah, Tannis. You're a gem. And a loyal friend to both Mary and me. Thanks for saving me from myself."

He raised a hand and brushed her cheek with a gentle finger, then turned and loped across the grass to his own door.

That night had never been mentioned again. And she'd never doubted Tom's love for Mary. As her illness had progressed, his devotion had been evident in the hours he'd spent tenderly caring for his wife.

After he left and Tannis was alone in the hot tub, she tried to relax. She honestly did. But all the enjoyment had gone out of the heated water. Grumbling under her breath, she grabbed for her towel and slung it around her as she mounted the steps. As she padded back across the concrete and entered her basement rec room, she glanced around the room, measuring the pile of dirty laundry spilling out of the basket and the hodgepodge of holiday decorations, tools and other miscellany with a critical eye. This would have sent Jeremy right into one of his famous fits.

He'd have lectured her on all her shortcomings—she caught herself short. It might be a mess, but she knew exactly where everything was and she knew it wasn't dirty because she'd vacuumed just last week. No, she wasn't about to allow anyone else's expectations to ruin her life ever again.

For the millionth time, she thought back to the heady days of infatuation and young love. She *had* loved Jeremy. Maybe that was why she'd excused his cold anger at her helter-skelter approach to housekeeping, his constant denigration and demands that she keep a spotless house. She'd run herself ragged trying to earn his approval in those days, only to find that she'd never done quite well enough, that he always found something lacking in her desperate attempts to please.

She'd die before she ever let a man destroy her self-esteem again.

On Thursday night, Tom stood inside his darkened living room. Amy and Jeb were in bed, and he was relaxing at the end of a long day. God, the days seemed endless now that he was a single parent.

Up at the crack of dawn to throw in a load of laundry, then an hour of exercise on the equipment in the basement before he got a shower, woke the kids and started breakfast. Most days he packed lunches while the kids ate and then he was off to the office after dropping them at Mrs. Cutter's. That would be one nice thing about having Tannis look after them. They could just walk next door and ride to school with her.

Tannis. He'd seen the happiness in her eyes when he'd extended the dinner invitation the other night, and he'd felt guilty. Hell, he *should* feel guilty. Amy and Jeb missed her, were always after him to let them go over to Tannis's house. It was one of the numerous sore spots between Amy and him these days. Every time Tannis so much as showed her head in the yard, his kids were out the door. He knew she cared for them, and he knew it was his fault for keeping them away from her. Once the numbness of losing his wife had worn off, the guilt had set in.

Ever since Tannis Anne Carlson had moved in next door, he'd been aware of her. He could still remember the first time he'd met her. Mary had already known her for over a week and had invited her to dinner to welcome her to the neighborhood. He'd seen her from a distance and had assessed her gently rounded figure like any red-blooded male would have, but nothing had prepared him for the petite copper-haired woman whose pouty lower lip and big brown eyes all but begged a man to follow her to the bedroom. When he took her hand, the force of her sensuality slammed into his gut and left him almost gasping. It had been all he could do to conceal the unexpected feeling from Mary, but he had. And he'd ignored it. Until that night . . .

God could never punish him as much as he'd punished himself for his lapse of control. On the other hand, he'd lost Mary. Maybe that *was* his punishment.

A movement on the concrete patio of the house next door grabbed his attention. Immediately his whole body clenched in anticipation. As Tannis emerged from the shadows, swathed in a huge, fluffy beach towel, he lectured himself.

This is low, Hayes, really low. Despicable. Disgusting. The poor woman thinks she's alone.

Tannis dropped the towel and mounted the steps to the hot tub. Tom's fingers clenched on the curtain. God, she was beautiful. Her waist was tiny, emphasizing the round curves of hip and buttock and the slender length of her legs, but it was her breasts that drew him. Large and rounded, they thrust proudly forward, the small darker circles of her nipples perfectly centered on each white globe. As she pivoted and dipped a toe in the water, they swayed gently.

Tom groaned aloud. The agonized sound echoed in the dark room and abruptly, he drew away from the curtains to slump against the wall beside the window, forcing himself to stop watching Tannis. This was crazy.

He dropped a hand to his sweatpants, then drew it away reluctantly. He could relieve his itch the easy way, but he knew from experience it wouldn't make him want Tannis any less.

It was just the sex, he told himself fiercely. He'd made love to Mary nearly every night of the ten years they'd been married. His mind might understand that Mary was gone but his body still reacted like it always had; it wanted a woman. And to make it worse, he'd tasted Tannis and he knew she could assuage his hunger. Simple sexual chemistry. That was all it was.

He'd loved his wife; he'd enjoyed sex with her. But Mary was gone, and he was still a man. A man with strong needs. About a month ago, he'd discovered that Tannis took hot tub dips in the buff. Since then, he'd been the worst sort of voyeur, watching in his darkened house every night just before nine when she usually appeared. She was driving him crazy.

Had she realized he could see beneath the water the other night? He didn't think so. It had been all he could do to keep his mind on the conversation when those pretty breasts had bobbed just below the water's surface, practically begging him to cup them with his hands.

He staggered over to the sofa and dropped down heavily. He couldn't look out that window one more time, or he'd go out there and join her. The very thought was enough to make his blood surge in painful anticipation. Okay, so he admitted it. He wanted to have sex with Tannis.

That didn't mean anything, he thought defensively. Though it was too dark to see her features, he stared at the rectangular shape of Mary's picture in the frame above the fireplace until his eyes burned painfully. He could almost hear her soft voice in his ear, could almost feel her slim curves pressed against his side. If she'd lived, he wouldn't be sitting here now, lusting after another woman. In fact, he'd probably be taking his wife to bed right this minute. A wave of grief tore through him. He was beginning to live with the loss much of the time now. But every once in a while, the raw pain of losing her caught him off guard.

Mixed with the pain was anger. He remembered the arguments, Mary's bullheaded refusal to heed the doctors' advice, the futile consultations with faith healers and herbalists. Why hadn't she at least *tried* to live? Much as he wished he could be noble, he'd never stop resenting the fact that Mary hadn't wanted to live for him, for their children. If she had accepted the conventional treatments the doctors had recommended, the radiation and chemotherapies, Mary might still be alive today.

And if Mary were alive, he wouldn't have this unquenchable thirst for Tannis.

Amy opened the door to Tannis's knock on Saturday evening. "Hi, Tannis!"

Tannis grinned. She couldn't help it. The twelve-year-old was wearing a denim skirt that was so short it barely peeked out from under her bright pink sweatshirt. The shirt was oversized in the current fashion; the arms hung down well over her fingertips. Lacy pink tights, heavy cotton socks scrunched around her ankles like fluffy weights, and tennis shoes completed the outfit, except for the gauzy scarf that floated out from her high ponytail.

"Hi, Amy. Nice outfit," she said dryly.

"Thanks." Amy beamed, missing the gentle sarcasm. "Dad says my skirt is too short, but he's just a *man,* you know?"

"Yeah, I know," Tannis responded.

"What do you think? Is it too short?"

Tannis tilted her head to one side and considered. "No, I think it's okay for twelve, but if you were thirteen or fourteen, I'd probably agree with your dad."

"You would?" Amy's face fell.

Tannis nodded. "It's a great look, especially since you have your mom's long legs. But once you get a little older and the boys start to notice you, it's wise to be more careful about how much of yourself you show them."

Amy looked thoughtful. "You mean I shouldn't wear stuff that's going to turn 'em on too much?"

"That's about it." Tannis held back startled laughter. A movement behind Amy caught her eye and she turned to see Tom standing in the doorway, a peculiar expression on his face. He didn't look mad, exactly, but more...penitent, almost, like Jebbie when he'd gotten sick from eating all those cookies he'd snitched at the Parent-Teacher Organization dinner. The look vanished before she could interpret it more accurately.

"Thanks," he said. "I've been trying to explain my concerns to her, but coming from Dopey Dad, it just doesn't sound the same."

To Tannis's surprise, a petulant look distorted Amy's pretty features. "Dad hates everything I wear."

Tannis didn't know what to say. Obviously this wasn't a good topic to pursue. "Dads worry about their little girls, honey. Sometimes moms and dads don't know how to explain the things that worry them."

Amy gave an exaggerated sniff and tossed her brown ponytail. "If that's true, then my dad must be the King of Worriers. My mom wouldn't have bugged me all the time about my clothes. She would have let me choose what I want to wear."

Tom's face registered the barb, but his tone was controlled. "Act your age, Ame. If you want to fight with me, save it for a time when we don't have company."

The young girl's face flushed scarlet, then she whirled and began pounding up the stairs. "I hate it when you treat me like a baby!" She vanished around the corner at the top of the steps and a moment later, a door slammed with resounding force.

Tannis stared after her, openmouthed. Holy cow. She'd never seen Amy behave like that before.

"Jeez." Tom sighed. Then he straightened and turned to face Tannis, and his green eyes were dark with regret. "Come on in. You don't have to act like company since you've just witnessed one of our daily encounters."

As Tannis followed Tom from the foyer back the hallway that led to the kitchen and family room, she ventured a comment. "I don't envy you a bit in the next few years. I remember my own adolescence all too well."

"You mean all girls act that way when they're growing up?" Tom shook his head as they entered the kitchen "Thank God boys' hormones don't affect them the same way. I'm not sure I could live through another Amy."

Perhaps a change of subject was in order, she thought. "Where's Jebbie?"

"Sue Sanderston on the next street over took him to swimming lessons. Her son, Miles, is in the same class."

"I know them. Nice people."

Tom looked relieved. "Good. Can you tell me anything about Charlie Swanson's family? He's invited Jeb over twice, but I didn't let him go because I never heard from the parents. I was going to ask you what you thought, since I figured you probably saw the kid around school."

She picked up a stack of plates and napkins sitting on the counter and walked toward the table with them.

"The little Swanson boy is a handful at school, which doesn't necessarily mean he wouldn't be a nice child, but I've heard some things about the family that would concern me if Jeb were my child. Maybe you could invite Charlie over here instead of letting Jebbie go there."

Tom didn't answer immediately, and she swiveled to see if he'd heard her. He was facing the kitchen cabinets with his hands pressed flat on the counter as if for support. His forehead was pressed against one of the wood cabinet doors and his eyes were closed.

"What's wrong?" she asked in alarm.

Two

—

Tom sighed heavily. "Single parenting is exhausting sometimes."

Though they'd been speaking of Jeb, she knew Tom's thoughts were of Amy. The girl was gone from the room but her resentment still lingered, a palpable presence in the air. Tannis was more disturbed by the scene she'd witnessed than she wanted him to know. "I imagine being the sole source of discipline makes for some tense moments with Amy. Try to remember it's just her age."

"Amy was such a happy little girl." Tom's fingers quivered under the strain of his tight grip on the counter. "She's turned into a stranger and I don't know how to talk to her anymore."

He sounded so defeated. Though she hadn't wanted to become involved in his problems with Amy, Tannis walked to his side and patted his hand in a gesture designed to comfort. The mild sizzle even that innocent touch produced caused her to yank her hand away as if his flesh were afire. She had to struggle to maintain her end of the conversation. "It's a stage almost all teenage girls go through—"

"But she's not even a teenager yet!" If Tom were affected by her touch, he gave no sign. He raked a hand through his curly dark hair. "She's only twelve years old and already she's hassling me about wearing nylons and makeup. I know the only reason she hasn't started bugging me for a bra is because she's too embarrassed to ask." He slanted her a look that held a glint of self-directed mockery in it. "Can you picture me showing Amy how to shave her legs?"

Despite the serious concern just below the surface of his light question, Tannis smiled. Then she caught his eye. "Why don't you let me help with at least two of those problems? I'd be happy to take Amy shopping for "feminine apparel" if you'd let her stay overnight with me some night. I'll do my best to teach her what to shave and how to accomplish it without cutting herself to bits...."

As she spoke, Tom had turned to look at her. Now she realized that he was no longer making any effort to meet her eyes. Instead, his own gaze was fastened on her mouth and her voice faltered into silence under the heated intensity of his gaze. Suddenly the conversation seemed stunningly intimate. What was Tom thinking?

Tannis cleared her throat. "I, uh, why don't I set the table? Smells as if dinner is almost ready."

Tom blinked. His eyes cleared and cooled, and she could see that he was suddenly uncomfortable with the degree of intimacy they'd been sharing. "Amy can do it. You're a guest."

Tannis shrugged. "Really, I don't mind—"

But he was already walking to the foot of the stairs. "Amy! Come set the table, please."

Tom strode back into the kitchen. Methodically he assembled salad ingredients and began chopping spinach into small chunks on an acrylic chopping block.

After a lengthy pause, Amy appeared again. She smiled at Tannis, studiously ignoring her father as she began to rattle and bang around in the drawer where the flatware was kept.

Tannis seized on the smile gratefully. There was nothing she hated worse than anger. Angry exchanges, even when they didn't involve her, invariably left her feeling tense and inadequate. "So how do you like school this year, Amy? I was pleased to see that you got Mrs. McCann for homeroom."

"School's okay." Amy's ponytail swung across her cheek as she came around the counter to the table. "Mr. Sykes is a dope, though. He wears a tie *every day!* I'm glad I don't have him for homeroom."

Tannis nearly chuckled at Amy's assessment of the sixth-grade math teacher. Instead, she offered what she hoped was a tactful smile. "Are you still taking piano lessons? I would enjoy hearing you play later."

To her chagrin, Amy's face settled into lines of discontent again. "Yeah, I'm still taking piano lessons. But I wish I wasn't. Piano's just...dumb, you know?"

Tannis hadn't missed the way the girl's gaze had darted to her father. Casually she said, "When I was in high school my best friend was the accompanist for the boys' chorus. She got all kinds of dates with those boys. Of course, I always wished I could have taken piano lessons, too."

Amy's eyebrows had risen in interest, but all she said was, "Well, you can take my place anytime."

Just then, the front door banged open and Jeb raced into the kitchen. "Tannis! Hi! Are you stayin' for supper?"

"Hi, Jeb. I sure am." Tannis greeted him with relief; she was beginning to regret giving in to the desire to join the Hayes family for dinner. "How have you been?"

"Good. Me 'n Miles took showers in the locker room all by ourselves today."

Tannis widened her eyes dramatically. "You're really growing up, aren't you?"

Jeb nodded emphatically with six-year-old assurance. "Yep." When he grinned, she could see a gap where he'd recently lost a tooth. He held up the battered mitt dangling from his left hand. "Look! I'm playing baseball this year. Today I got a hit every time I came up to bat."

Amy sniffed. "Big deal. Anybody can hit a dumb ball when it's sitting right there on a tee in front of 'em."

"Can not!" Jeb's lower lip came out and his voice immediately assumed a belligerent tone.

"I agree with you, Jeb." Tannis drew him against her side and buffed her hand across the top of his short, trendy haircut, while over his head she gave

Amy an exaggerated wink, hoping the teenager would buy into being treated like an adult. "I'm a terrible ball player. I could never make a hit every time I came up to bat."

To her relief, Amy smiled back conspiratorially, and the tense atmosphere in the kitchen lightened as Tannis chatted with the children until Tom approached the table with a casserole dish.

Quickly he and Amy assembled the rest of the food, then they all sat down together. The meal wasn't fancy, but Tom had done a fine job with the chicken casserole and a spinach salad with some kind of tasty dressing.

"Wow. Where did you learn to cook?" Tannis asked.

His gaze was sober as it met hers across the table. "I can read cookbooks."

"Yeah," Amy chimed in. "About a year ago, I told Dad I'd start to cook if he would."

"We were getting awful sick of hot dogs," Jeb said.

Tom shrugged. "I like hot dogs."

"So do we," Amy said, shaking her head as if he were hopeless, but her glance at her father was fond. "But not every night, Dad."

After supper, Tannis cajoled the children into helping Tom clean up the dishes, then they all sat down to play a board game, which Amy won, much to Jeb's disgust. Then they switched to a simple card game that was one of Jeb's favorites. After Jeb won hands down and crowed loudly over the fact, Tom sent the children upstairs to get ready for bed.

She wished the kids didn't have to go to bed. Jeb and Amy provided a buffer between Tom and her, a way to avoid discussing anything serious. She knew he was going to ask her to make a decision about the job he'd offered her, and she knew he wasn't going to like what he heard.

She wandered around the room while he told the children good-night, stopping to look at the magazines and various kinds of books that were scattered everywhere. Tom's voice stopped her in her tracks.

"Have you made a decision about watching the kids?"

She nodded without turning around. "I have, but—"

"They're well behaved most of the time. Amy seems to reserve her hostile moments for me. They wouldn't cause any major problems. And I'd certainly feel better having them stay with someone I know I can trust."

She felt terrible. She wanted to be able to do it, both to ease his mind and to ease her own conscience about that promise she'd made to Mary. And because she cared for Amy and Jeb. But it just wasn't possible.

"Tom, I can't," she said, turning to face him squarely, shaking her head before he could elaborate further. "I wish I could—you know I'd love to keep them—but I can't."

"Why not?" There was an aggressive tilt to his jaw that she knew meant he hadn't given up yet.

She sighed. She was going to have to tell him all of it. "I need a second job," she said slowly.

"All right! Then this—"

"No. You don't understand. I'm going to have to get an evening and weekend job that will give me lots of hours. I need more income than I could make babysitting for you."

Tom didn't speak for a long time. She could hear the brass mantel clock ticking loudly into the silence. Finally he asked, "Why do you need money so badly?"

She twined her fingers together, looking down at them rather than at him. "My mother had to move into a nursing home three years ago. She has a severe arthritic condition, which has gotten much worse in the past few years. She just couldn't manage on her own anymore."

"Didn't she have any savings? Money from the sale of a house?" Tom was always logical, seeking all the practical angles.

"Yes, to both, but they didn't amount to much. She's just about exhausted all her money."

"And you're footing the bill now."

"Yes."

"There are less costly alternatives, Tannis. Have you shopped around for price comparisons? Perhaps she—"

"I couldn't do that to her," she said impatiently. "This place is nice. It's clean, it doesn't smell bad like so many of the other places we visited, and there are a number of other fairly young senior citizens like Mom. Besides, I can't imagine what another move would do to her. It was terribly difficult for her to part with our old house and most of her things the first time."

"So why doesn't her medical coverage pay?" Tom wasn't giving up. The jaw still clued her in to his determination.

"It does. But not everything."

"Have you considered moving her in here with you? You certainly have plenty of room."

Did she catch a note of censure in his voice? The idea of him judging her when he really knew nothing about it didn't sit well. "My mother and I have had some differences of opinion in the past. I don't think she'd be happy leaving Culpeper and frankly, I don't think I could take having her living with me."

Tom was silent again. The air in the room suddenly seemed oppressive, accusatory. He didn't say a word but the look on his face said it all.

She wasn't used to having to explain herself. Besides, what did she care what he thought? But his disapproval rankled, and her discomfort grew until she blurted. "Don't you dare judge me, Tom Hayes. You have no idea what my life was like with her. After I left my husband, my mother was furious with me. She said I was a poor excuse for a daughter if I just up and quit a marriage because of a little misunderstanding."

"Tannis—" Tom was shaking his head.

"Do you know I almost went back to Jeremy because she made me feel like such a failure? It wasn't enough that Jeremy already had taken my self-esteem and my confidence and—and my love. Even when his second marriage broke up last year, my mother wasn't willing to back down. Every time I visit, she gets in some little crack about my shortcomings in the marriage mart." Bitterly, she shook her head and turned away as she felt treacherous tears sting her eyes. She wouldn't cry. She *would not cry* in front of him.

Then Tom's hands came down on her shoulders, and she jumped. She'd never heard him move. "Tannis." His voice was husky as he turned her around.

She was so aware of his large body only inches from hers, and the heat that flowed from his hands into her shoulders and body, that she could barely attend to his words.

"I'm sorry. I didn't mean to give you the impression I thought you owed it to your mother to bring her here. Mary told me about your marriage. You were right to leave."

His hands slid down her arms and linked with her fingers, and she had to lock her knees to keep from sinking to the floor. Her heart began to thud, and she felt the blood rushing through her veins. Why did Tom affect her so strongly? His green eyes were so dark and intense she couldn't sustain the contact and she looked away, down at the floor. But that was a mistake because there was only a tiny amount of floor visible between their bodies—a tiny space that could be closed so effortlessly.

"I won't press you about the baby-sitting again," he told the top of her head. "I understand why you need to find a job that can pay you more."

Tannis slid her hands free of his. If she allowed him to continue touching her, she wouldn't be responsible for her actions. "Thank you." She had a catch in her throat and she cleared it nervously as she looked back up at him. "I have a favor to ask of you now."

One of Tom's eyebrows slid up in inquiry.

"Would you be willing to act as a reference for me?" The words tumbled out in a rush. "You've known me longer than anyone else in this area and I'm going to need references for prospective employers."

"I'd be happy to be a reference for you," he told her, and his voice was even deeper than its usual bass tones. A considering look passed across his features.

Not a smile, exactly, but a warm expression that sent little skitters of unease chasing down her spine.

"Tom?" she prompted. "What's the matter?"

"Not a thing." A silver gleam lit his eyes. "Do you remember the night I kissed you?"

Heat streaked through her. She was stunned. Of all the things she'd expected he might say, that wasn't even on the list.

"I've thought about that kiss for years." His voice was a rough growl as he went on. "I think I'm going to have to find out whether we're as good together as I remember."

Automatically she opened her mouth to protest, to ask him to repeat what he'd said. But before she could rally her paralysed vocal cords, Tom slid his arms around her in one smooth motion, closing that tiny gap she'd fantasized over only moments before.

Her breath caught in shock as she felt his strong, firm body pressed against hers and his mouth came down to cover her lips. For a moment she was quiet beneath his hands, her lips unresponsive to the demand of his. Then, as the daze of shock passed, she was electrified by sensation, acutely aware of the hard possession of his lips, the scrape of beard stubble against her chin, the massive plane of his chest pressing against her, his belt buckle digging into her torso.

Dear God. This was no hasty kiss regretted almost before it had concluded. This was every fantasy she'd had of Tom since that first kiss, every erotic thought that had passed through her mind before she could expunge it and remind herself that he was her best friend's husband. Flash fires of sensation assailed her nerve endings. As the scent of hot man mingled with his cologne and the warmth of his big body surrounded her, she gave in to the urgent desire to know him fully, sinking against him in limp surrender, lifting her arms to link them around his neck.

As if he sensed how complete her yielding was, Tom shifted her in his embrace, using one muscled arm to support her while the other stroked surely down over her back to her bottom, cupping her and lifting her into even greater contact with him. She could feel his arousal, impossibly hard and heavy where it pressed against her belly; her own excitement spiraled higher as he gripped her bottom intimately. When he aggressively changed the slant of his mouth over hers, she met him mindlessly, opening her lips to allow him entrance, exchanging deep, searching kisses, mating her mouth with his in wild abandon as if they'd known each other intimately every day rather than twice in eight years. She slipped one hand up into his hair, cradling his scalp, and a part of her registered the surprisingly silky texture of his dark locks as he crushed them between her fingers.

Tom groaned. The hand at her back slipped beneath her sweater while his other hand slid even farther down her leg until he was clasping the back of her thigh. Dimly she realized he was urging her leg up and around him. Like a climbing vine that would collapse without support, she hooked her leg around his and allowed him to angle his body into the wide V of her legs. His blatant seduction of her mouth became even more urgent, and his powerful body surged repeatedly against her, rocking her back and forth against him.

She never thought of refusing him. For years she'd bottled up the longings she'd felt for him, refusing to acknowledge the potency of the last time he'd touched her. Ever since that one moment of weakness, she'd denied that he was anything more than an attractive man who happened to be married to a woman who'd become very dear to her.

Tannis was wrenched from the warm cascade of sensual heat searing her by the unaccustomed pleasure/pain of a man's hard hand roughly caressing her breast. As the clouds of passion momentarily parted, she realized Tom had lifted her sweater and freed one breast from the scant protection of her bra. Despite the lightning bolts of pure sexual desire licking through her, a great alarm sounded inside her head.

"Stop!" What was she doing? Frantically she unhitched her leg from its close embrace and pulled away from him, grasping his wrist and trying to force his hand from her body. "Tom, you have to stop," she hissed.

"Why?" His voice was a low rasp in her ear. She turned her head to avoid his seeking mouth, but he wouldn't be deterred. He simply seized her earlobe in his warm mouth and began to nuzzle and tease the sensitive shell.

Tannis sank her fingers into his hair, tugging forcefully until she'd pulled his mouth a safe distance from her. "Because this isn't wise."

Unfortunately, with her hands occupied, his were free and he immediately slipped them down her back and pulled her against him again. They both sucked in a startled breath at the thrill of the tight fit, and Tom uttered a short, harsh laugh. "Feels like the wisest thing I've done in a long time."

"You know what I mean," she insisted. She felt totally exposed, gazing into his eyes as she was, and some odd, detached part of her noticed that his irises weren't simply green, as they appeared from a distance, but full of rich flecks of bronze, black and gold, as well as piercing emerald.

Tom shifted her over him once, and his gaze dropped to her mouth. "Why are we wasting time talking? Kiss me again, Tannis."

Though she thrilled to the sound of her name on his lips, she still shook her head, trying desperately to free herself from the near-hypnotized state he induced. "No. We'd be crazy to get involved."

Her words seemed to strike a chord in him and he lifted his gaze to hers again. The cool reserve in that look chilled her to the bone. "Who said anything about getting involved? I want you. You want me. A straightforward sexual relationship would be good for both of us. No emotions, but no risks, either." His voice was persuasive and he flashed her a roguish grin that made her heart skip a beat, though his eyes remained watchful. "It would be the perfect arrangement."

He dropped his head and kissed her again with all his considerable skill, but he'd destroyed the mindlessness of the moment and Tannis didn't respond. His words had struck a raw spot. She'd lived without love in her life since she'd walked away from her marriage with her ego in shreds. She'd stayed busy for the past few years, too much so to allow herself to think much about the future. But having him say it made the whole issue unavoidable any longer. To love would require that she trust again, that she give her heart. And she didn't think that was possible. She couldn't survive having her dreams crushed a second time.

But when she looked down the long, empty vista that was her future, her heart shriveled in pain at the thought of never having a family. Never bearing a baby, never knowing the thrill of raising a child of her own. Growing old alone, enduring solitary holidays for the rest of her life. No, she couldn't truly say that she wanted to be alone. Maybe there was someone out there like her, someone who didn't want to have to give his heart. Someone who would be content with friendship and affection and warm, comforting sex.

Someone who wouldn't tempt her to fall in love with him. With a terrible clarity, she suddenly recognized how very vulnerable she was to this man. He could make her feel things better left behind. Tom Hayes could get into her heart . . . and he could break it.

Wrenching herself away from him, she took several rapid steps across the room before she turned to face him again. "No, Tom, it wouldn't be the perfect arrangement. Not for me."

Pivoting swiftly, she made her way through the darkened kitchen and took her coat from the front hall. Tom didn't come after her, and she suppressed the stupid corner of her mind that played out a fantasy of him begging her to stay and overpowering her feeble resistance with tender strength.

She often went for a walk after supper. Ever since the weekend, when the desire between them had flared out of control again, he'd taken to watching her house like a stalker in a late-night movie. He knew she'd be wary of him after what had happened between them, but he was determined to establish contact with her again.

He'd always followed his instincts when he was deeply involved in a case and he had a similar feeling about Tannis. But he wasn't about to examine his reasons too closely.

On the Thursday night after the fateful dinner invitation, Amy and Jeb each had gone to a friend's house. Tom casually opened his front door and strolled across the lawn when he saw her coming out in her walking sneakers and sweats. As he walked up to her, she stopped dead and he saw panic and puzzlement flash through her blue eyes before she cast him a measured smile.

"Good evening, Tom."

"Hi. Mind if I join you? I saw you coming out to walk and thought I could use the exercise, too."

"I don't mind." But she didn't make eye contact. "I thought you used your rowing machine and free weights in the mornings."

Hell. Claiming he needed the exercise had been stupid. She knew too much about him. "I still work out. It's nice getting up early and having that hour to myself before the rat race begins." He went on digging himself out of the hole. "We had a big dinner tonight and I needed to walk it off."

She still stood in her driveway regarding him with that somewhat puzzled smile. Finally, to get her moving, he took her elbow and started down the asphalt toward the street. She immediately put at least a foot of space between them.

They walked at a brisk pace that guaranteed to burn a few calories. No wonder every inch of her had felt so firm underneath his palms the other night. He already knew from timing her the past few nights that these jaunts usually lasted a good fifty minutes.

He cast a surreptitious glance at her and was captivated by the way her breasts jiggled beneath the purple-and-gold James Madison University sweatshirt. No, jiggled wasn't the right word. They bounced. Softly, gently, in rhythm with her footsteps, they bounced to the right, then to the left . . . he thought women wore sport bras to prevent that these days. Then again, maybe she already *was* wearing one. His imagination reconstructed a mental image of her rising from her hot tub and he had to concede that a sport bra would be hard-pressed to contain the full loveliness of the bosom he'd seen.

Despite the vigorous exercise, he felt his body begin to respond to his fantasizing. Oops, better occupy his mind before she looked at him and noticed he was drooling.

"Remember I asked you about Charlie Swanson and you told me to invite him over?"

She arched her eyebrows. "I don't recall phrasing it quite like that. What I said was that you might invite him over rather than allowing Jeb to go to his home." Her eyes danced. "Did you?"

Tom nodded. He felt his own lips twitch. "Yeah. Little Charlie's a bit of a dynamo, isn't he?"

"A bit." She laughed. "Did he trash your house?"

"I sent them to play in the basement," he reported. Thank God she seemed to be relaxing with him again.

"When I heard a couple of really big crashing noises I went down to see what was going on."

"And?"

"Every single toy on the shelves in the playroom was piled in the middle of the floor. Jeb and Charlie were pretending to be paratroopers jumping from the top shelf with pillowcases for parachutes."

Her eyes were big and round. "What did you do?"

Tom smiled grimly. "Charlie had a lesson in helping with family cleanup before he went home. But that isn't all. When I put Jeb in the bathtub later, he was playing with his plastic army men, making them speak, and I heard him utter a few choice words."

"Like what?" She was laughing aloud now.

He told her.

"You're kidding!"

"Nope. He told me Charlie says them."

"Where do you suppose that little boy learned *those?*"

Tom shook his head. "I shudder to think what that kid's home life must be like."

She made a noise of agreement. "What did you do?"

He spread his hands. "I told Jeb real men didn't need to use those kinds of words to be tough, that they were for sissies."

She nodded approvingly. "Interesting approach."

"Then I told him I'd blister his backside if I ever heard him saying anything like that again."

That startled another giggle out of her. He realized he was enjoying talking to her, enjoying the warm atmosphere between them. He just might make these evening walks a ritual. Of course, if she got a night job, she wouldn't be able to walk in the evening. That prompted him to ask, "How's the job search going?"

Almost immediately, he wished he hadn't. Her face fell and he could see her shoulders slump. "I found work. I start at Johnnie's Seafood Emporium this weekend."

"As a waitress?"

"Not at first. I'll work as a hostess for a few months and eventually, they'll train me to wait tables. That's what I'm hoping for because Johnnie's does a good business and some of the girls I talked to do pretty well in tips."

"You're going to have your hands full working two jobs." He tried hard not to let on how horrified he was. She was going to be exhausted.

"I know." Her voice was morose. "But there's no help for it."

They walked for a few minutes in silence, then she asked him about the cases he was working on presently. He told her about the two women—sisters—who had showed up in his office last week to discuss the disbursement of their mother's estate.

"The mother is one of my clients," he explained. "I was a little surprised that I hadn't learned of her passing away, but I figured it was possible. When I expressed my condolences, the older one said, 'Oh, no, Mr. Hayes, Mama hasn't kicked off yet. We just want to be sure we have everything divvied up fair and square when she does!'"

Tannis looked shocked. "I hope you advised that poor old woman to give all her money to the Society for the Protection of Humpbacked Whales or something. Those two don't deserve a penny!''

"It's a tempting thought." Tom smiled as a memory struck him. "Mary used to do some filing for me when I first opened my practice. She used to read all the papers she was supposed to be filing and she'd get so indignant over some of the cases that I'd have to restrain her from marching off to some client's house and berating him for leaving his wife and four dependents." He shook his head. "I finally had to ban her from the office!''

Tannis nodded. "I can see that. She always had so much energy. I remember the year she was president of the Parent-Teacher Organization, chairman of the church's fund-raising campaign and the coordinator of Amy's play group. She used to tell me she felt like a juggler barely keeping all the balls in the air.''

"She loved to be busy like that. She lived on the edge of organizational insanity." Funny how he could bear to talk about Mary with Tannis.

"I was one of her unofficial projects when we first met." Her voice was full of wry fondness. "She was determined to drag me out of the antisocial shell I'd adopted after my divorce.''

"She did give it her best shot," he agreed. "Remember the dinner party where she invited you and that guy over on the next street who had the nine cats? I'll never forget the glazed look in your eyes as he droned on and on about Miss Muffet's hair ball problem and how much he spent on special food for his male cat with the, uh, bladder problem.''

"As I recall, you rescued me," she reminded him. "You told him I was allergic to cat dander.''

Tom was smiling again. "He left ten minutes later."

"I don't think I ever said thank you for that."

"Yes, you did." His good mood evaporated in an instant. "When Mary got sick, I don't know what I'd have done without you. You took care of the kids, you helped with housework, you entertained Mary when I was so burned-out I could barely think."

"I didn't do—"

"You did," he said again. "You were there for us, Tannis. Mary couldn't have asked for a better friend. Neither could I."

It seemed there was nothing more to be said after that. They finished the walk in silence, and she hurried into her house with barely a goodbye.

He wanted to call her back, to ask her to go out with him, but he knew she'd refuse. He'd been clumsy the week before, trying to use her physical response to him, and only moments earlier, he thought he'd overcome his blunder and lowered some of her defenses.

Now it seemed he was back at the starting gate again.

Three

Two months later, Tannis wearily gathered up the papers she'd brought home to grade and stuffed them back into the book bag she carried to and from school every day. She glanced at the clock—almost time to go to Job Number Two. If she hurried, she could make a sandwich and eat it while she put on her hostess uniform.

Nah. Too much trouble. She wasn't hungry, anyway. As she trudged up the stairs, she reflected that loss of appetite was the only good thing about working two jobs. It kept her too busy to eat. She'd lost almost ten pounds in the past eight weeks and her figure had melted down to a svelte shape a full size smaller than she'd been wearing. She liked it. Who cared if several of her colleagues had told her she was getting too thin?

Her hostess uniform smelled like seafood, even though she religiously hand-washed it each one of the four nights she worked during the week. When she came home from the restaurant on Saturdays, she threw it into the washing machine. She looked in the mirror after she'd dressed. The burgundy shade of the jumper was truly awful with her hair. She had to be careful about wearing any colors in the red family, and this was one of those unfortunate shades that made her wince when she viewed the combination. But there was nothing she could do about it. The manager of the restaurant had chosen those uniforms just weeks before she'd been hired, and all the staff had to wear them.

Oh well, it wasn't as if she had anyone to impress.

Forty minutes later, she buzzed through the swinging door from the kitchen with a large tray of iced shrimp, which she placed in one of the glass-fronted display counters. Absently she rubbed her temples, struggling to focus on her next task despite the ache in her head. The raw feeling in the back of her throat warned her that she was probably catching a cold, but she didn't have time to worry about it. A hasty glance at the door assured her that there were no customers approaching to be seated or checked out, so she grabbed an empty tub and went to bus a table in one of the back sections. She cleared the table, set it with fresh linens and table service and was ringing up someone's bill when the door opened to admit new customers.

She glanced up with an automatic smile plastered in place, but it froze on her face when she saw Tom standing before her.

"Hi, Tom. Welcome to Johnnie's Seafood. I'll be with you in a moment," she managed to recite before she turned back to finish the transaction with the two older ladies waiting for their change. Her fingers were as clumsy as if she were wearing thick gloves, and she could feel waves of fiery color sweeping up her neck. Of all the rotten luck...!

She hadn't seen him since the evening he'd walked with her—except on a few occasions when one of them had been climbing in or out of a car. But she'd dreamed of him several times, erotic dreams from which she woke feeling lonely and dissatisfied and, if she were honest, incredibly sexually frustrated. For the millionth time, she cursed him mentally, enraged anew that he had destroyed what little peace she'd managed to make for herself. Before Tom had kissed her again, she'd been able to tell herself she didn't want, didn't need a man in her life.

She couldn't even think it now without superstitiously crossing her fingers to prevent a lightning bolt from sizzling her into a small, smoking pile of ash.

She finished ringing out the ladies. Then she rounded the hostess station, efficiently gathering a menu as she approached Tom with her smile firm and her shaking fingers carefully hidden. "Just one? I have a table this way." Indicating the direction she would take him, Tannis turned away.

"Tannis." Tom grasped her elbow. "This is ridiculous."

"What is?" The warmth of his fingers seared her flesh through the fabric of her uniform blouse, reinforcing the leaping awareness she was struggling to banish. She tried to tug her arm away from him, keeping her voice low so they wouldn't attract attention, but he wouldn't let her go. Short of engaging in a tug-of-war for possession of her body, she wasn't going to get away from his firm grip. One of the waitresses shot her a speculative look as she breezed by.

Tom increased his hold on her arm. "This waitressing is ridiculous."

"I'm a hostess, not a waitress. And I think I do a decent job. It's not ridiculous at all." She moved toward the table she'd shown him, and Tom followed, still grasping her elbow.

"Stupidity doesn't become you," he said, standing in her path when she would have seen him into a seat and retreated. "You've lost weight and you have dark circles under your eyes. You have to be exhausted. You can't keep this up."

She'd thought the very same thing, but her chin came up at the authoritative tone of his voice. "I don't consider taking care of my family stupid. Besides, I don't have a choice."

"Let me make you a low-interest loan," he said.

She shook her head impatiently. "How long would that last? I need permanent income." She glanced over her shoulder to where the manager had come out of the kitchen to stare pointedly at her from behind the register. "Sit down and let me go. You're going to get me in trouble."

"I only want to help," he said. He released her and slid into the seat, but when she turned to go, he circled her wrist with long fingers, holding her in place again. "You helped us. Why not let me help you?"

A door of revelation opened in her mind at his words. So that was it. He still was trying to pay her back for her devotion to Mary through her illness. Why did she find the thought so depressing?

More sharply than she'd intended, she said, "I don't want your help. Anything I did for Mary, I did because I loved her. The last thing I'd accept is a reward from you."

The words hung in the air for a moment. Tom's eyes took on a hard emerald edge, and slowly he released her wrist. His voice, when he finally spoke, was so cool and deep that she understood instantly that she'd crossed some invisible line and offended him mortally. "My mistake," he said. "Consider the offer withdrawn."

She couldn't get the memory of her last encounter with Tom out of her head. But as the week passed, her cold blossomed into a raging illness that took all her strength to combat. The following Thursday, Tannis dragged herself home from school and slumped down on the couch in her living room. Her satchel was full of ungraded student work that she really ought to start on, but she was due at the restaurant in ninety minutes and she felt so awful...maybe she'd feel better if she took a short nap before she went in to work.

Slowly she climbed the stairs. Her head was pounding and her throat was raw. She'd been experiencing alternating periods of freezing and being too warm all afternoon. Scrounging in the medicine cabinet, she downed a cold medicine that contained pain reliever and scurried under the covers, then fumbled her way upright again to set her alarm clock for four-thirty. That would give her half an hour to dress and make the short drive to the restaurant.

When she awoke, the first thing she noticed was that her room was dark. Dark? A bolt of panic shot through her and she threw back the sheet, but when she sat up, the room spun around her. She moaned and put out a hand. When it encountered the smooth, cool wood of the bedpost, she merely sat for a moment with her eyes closed until the feeling of motion passed. Cautiously she opened her eyes.

The digital alarm read 8:22.

Eight twenty-two!

"Oh, no!" She was scheduled to work at five. What could have happened to her alarm?

Completely panicked, Tannis frantically donned her uniform and splashed water on her face. Her head was aching, and an odd disorientation forced her to walk with one hand on the wall for balance as she moved through the house, but all she could think of was getting to work. In some part of her mind, she recognized that her single-minded focus wasn't quite rational, but her thoughts were too chaotic to allow the idea to surface.

Getting into the car was almost a relief. Sitting down helped banish the spinning sensation a little. She pulled into a parking space at the restaurant moments later and quickly ran across the parking lot to the employee door. She had to pause and lean against the outside wall until the world stopped its crazy gyrations; then she took a deep breath and stepped inside.

Everything would be all right now that she was at work.

As she hung her coat on a hook against the wall and locked her pocketbook in the closet, one of the waitresses came rushing into the kitchen with an order.

When she turned from posting it for the chef, she
caught sight of Tannis.

Her mouth fell open. "Where the heck have you
been?"

"I overslept." To Tannis's amazement, her voice
came out a croak. She hadn't tried to speak since she'd
come home from school; now her throat felt so swollen she barely could squeeze out a sound.

"Watch out for Lew, he's pretty mad at you." The
young woman flung the words over her shoulder as she
balanced another tray of entrées on an upraised hand
and rushed back through the swinging door to the
dining room.

Tannis grimaced. If she could just get through this
evening, she'd ask Lew to replace her tomorrow evening, call in sick at school tomorrow and stay in bed
all day. Slowly, staying close to the wall for balance,
she edged toward the door that led to the hostess station and the front take-out counter.

Just before she walked through the door, it swung
forcefully inward and Lew, the manager, came burst-
ing into the kitchen. "Where do you think you're going?" he demanded, stopping right in front of her and
blocking her way with his flabby frame.

"I—Lew, I'm sorry." She listened in horrified
amazement to the froglike quality of her own voice.
"I've been sick and I overslept. I—"

"You *overslept?*" Lew's round face was almost
purple with rage. "The waitresses are shorthanded
because they had to bus their own tables tonight, the
kitchen staff is running forty minutes behind on orders because I've been seating people and ringing them

out so I couldn't be helping them and you were sleeping?"

"I'm sorry," she repeated. "It won't happen again—"

"Damn right it won't." Lew spat the words at her. "I need people I can depend on. You're finished lady. Off the schedule as of tomorrow."

"Lew!" Tannis cried, aghast. "I need this job. I'm really sorry. Please. It will never happen again."

But the manager had already turned away. "I got work to do. Bring your uniform in tomorrow and your final check will be waiting." And he shoved through the swinging door to the front.

She stood for a frozen moment, unable to believe his words. Finally the situation began to penetrate her thick brain. *She'd been fired!* Oh, God, what was she going to do? She crossed the kitchen and fumbled with the outside door, but a wave of dizziness assailed her and she had to lean her head against the cool metal for a minute.

"Hey! Tannis, wait. Don't forget your coat." It was the chef, his face sympathetic as he held out her forgotten coat and purse. "Lew's a mean ol' critter. He never gives anybody second chances. One mistake and you're canned." The chef's powerful arms bustled her into her coat and patted the strap of her pocketbook on her shoulder. "You look like hell, kid. Go on home and get better. You don't need this job."

"But I do," Tannis mumbled as she crossed the parking lot and slid into her aging compact car. "I do need this job." As she put the car in gear, silent tears began to roll down her cheeks. Her mortgage payment was coming due and she'd been counting on the income she'd make through the weekend to pay it. And the phone bill was nearly past due. And she had to start saving for taxes. Thank goodness she'd just sent off a hefty check to her mother's nursing home.

But where would she get the money for next month?

The tears increased and her shoulders began to shake. Deep, harsh sobs tore out of her sore throat. Her head pounded and she had trouble seeing the lines on Route 29 as she drove out of the city toward home.

It was with great relief that she turned into her community and finally lurched her car to a halt in her driveway.

Tom's house was near the bottom of a lane that ended in a circle. Few cars came up and down the quiet street. He was in his home office, reviewing the will of an older client who had just passed away.

Or at least, he was trying to concentrate on work, he amended. He'd been having no trouble until he'd seen Tannis come out of her house and drive away. Seeing her fold her slender body into her little car had brought back graphic, fiery sensations of that body pressed against his as he kissed her.

And she'd kissed him back. The mere memory was enough to make beads of sweat stand out on his forehead. He got hard every time he thought of the way she'd wrapped herself around him and returned his intimate caresses with her tongue. What would they be like together without clothes to impede them? He already knew what a beautiful body she had. Hell, he'd even had his hands on her, though he'd only seen her naked from a distance.

And, judging from the way she'd reacted, he'd probably never get any closer than that again. Amy would see a lot more of Tannis than he was likely to. He recalled Tannis's generous offer to teach Amy how to shave her legs. He hadn't been able to answer her for a minute, because all he could think of was the silky smooth length of Tannis's legs and how they'd feel wrapped around his hips. Then he'd had the sudden, stupid fear that Mary might be monitoring his thoughts from wherever she was now, that she'd be awfully disappointed in her husband's lecherous thoughts.

Oh, he didn't think that Mary would object to him finding someone else to share his life. She'd been so warm and loving that he knew she'd approve. But making a commitment to an unknown woman was a lot different than lusting after Tannis, whom Mary had loved dearly. And lust he did.

Maybe that was why he'd gotten so damned mad when Tannis had thrown that line at him in the restaurant about not needing his help. He beat back the anger and reached for patience. Didn't she understand he hadn't meant it as a reward for her steadfast care for Mary? Though God knew she deserved it for that alone. But that hadn't been his motive. He'd genuinely only been thinking of Tannis when he'd made the offer, worrying about how she could manage without his help.

But she'd thrown his help back in his face. Just as Mary had. Mary hadn't been as blunt, but still, she'd refused to try any of his frantic suggestions and had done exactly what she wanted. And she'd died.

A car passed his house. Automatically, he glanced up. His desk faced the front of the house. He'd left the miniblinds open, and his gaze suddenly sharpened when he recognized the clanking sound of Tannis's car.

And she didn't have her headlights on!

Why wasn't she at work? And what the hell was she doing driving around with no lights? It was full dark, had been for hours. He pushed his chair away from the desk and went to the window, watching as she pulled her car into her driveway and stopped with a sharp jerk. He had half a mind to go over there and ream her out.

As he stood, deliberating, Tannis opened the door of her car, stood up—

And slumped to the ground beside the car.

My God! Had she been in an accident? That could explain the lack of lights. Tom rushed into the front hallway and yanked open his front door. He was across the lawn and on his knees beside her before he could consciously give his body a command to move. His heart was racing, his pulse roaring in his ears. She looked undamaged. What was wrong with her? Illness terrified him. Ever since Mary, he'd leapt to have Jeb's or Amy's every sniffle diagnosed . . . he knew it wasn't entirely rational, but he didn't feel very rational when he thought about his kids becoming ill.

Seeing Tannis collapse produced that same dry-mouthed, panicky feeling.

"Tannis?" Gently he pressed his fingers to her wrist and was elated to feel a pulse. But she didn't respond. Her chest rose and fell slightly, so she was breathing, and none of her limbs looked unnaturally twisted.

When he lifted an eyelid to check her pupils, she groaned and rolled onto her side, against his knees.

"Tannis, it's Tom. Talk to me. What's wrong?"

"Sick," she muttered, and he was appalled at how strained her voice sounded. Then she said, "Just a cold."

He was simultaneously relieved and even more concerned. She was conscious—but it was plain to him that she had far more than a cold. Aloud he said, "Let's get you into your house."

She didn't answer, but when he slipped one arm beneath her knees and the other beneath her back, she feebly passed an arm around his neck. Her head fell against his shoulder and a great wave of protectiveness washed through him. He would take care of her.

He strode up her driveway to the front door, pausing when he realized he had no key. "Where's your house key?" he asked her, bending his head down. Her forehead brushed his lips, and he realized with a start of fear that she was burning up with fever.

"In . . . my purse." The words were slurred and he began to feel frantic. He had to call a doctor and get that fever down. Kneeling, he held her against him with one hand while with the other he rummaged through the pocketbook that dangled from her shoulder. Hefting her again, he inserted the key into the lock and breathed a sigh of relief when it swung open. He shouldered his way into the room, carrying Tannis directly up the darkened stairs. When he got to the top, he flipped on the hallway light with his elbow.

Her room was easy to find. It was the only one with a bed. Careful not to jostle her unnecessarily, Tom lay her down. She was soft and warm, and the sweet scent of woman rose to tease him as he straightened and sat at her side. Impatient with his awareness of her, he picked up the telephone that rested on the bedside table. The first call was to a college student down the street who still lived at home. Antha agreed to come and stay with his kids, and he told her to bring her books because Amy and Jeb were already asleep.

Then he bent over Tannis. "Who's your doctor?" he asked her.

Her eyelids fluttered and her mouth moved, but it was a moment before she responded. "Dr. Ellis. At the Family Health Clinic in the shopping center."

He hadn't known that. It was a stroke of luck, because Ellis was his family's physician as well. Dr. Ellis had suspected Mary's cancer and sent her to a specialist right away. Not that it had done any good, since Mary had refused to take any sensible advice—catching himself, he closed a mental door on the bitter thoughts. Tannis needed his full attention right now.

"I'll be back in a minute," he told her, though she didn't indicate that she'd even heard him.

First he ran next door and got his keys and jacket. The baby-sitter knocked a moment later and he let her in with instructions to lock the door behind him and call him next door if she needed him.

Then he went back to Tannis's house. He called Dr. Ellis's answering service and left an urgent message for the doctor to call Tannis's house. Going into the attached bathroom, he opened her medicine cabinet, wondering if he dared give her any medication.

As he stood pondering the meager supply of cold medicine and pain reliever, the phone rang and he ran for it before it could disturb Tannis.

"Hello?"

"This is Dr. Ellis calling for Tannis Carlson."

Thank God. "Hi, Dr. Ellis. This is Tom Hayes. I'm Tannis's neighbor."

"Is something wrong with Tannis?" the doctor asked.

"She says she has a cold," Tom reported. "But she's running a high fever, she's wheezing when she breathes and she's so hoarse she can barely speak. She fainted in her driveway a few minutes ago."

"Has she been sick long?"

"I don't know. I went outside when I saw her fall. What should I do?" Tom heard the desperation rising in his voice and apparently the doctor did, too, because he said, "Stay calm, Tom. Tannis sounds pretty sick but I don't think her life is in danger. I could come to the house, but I would prefer to see her at the clinic where I have more supplies. Can she be moved?"

"I can be at the clinic in five minutes."

"I don't live far. I'll meet you there," Dr. Ellis assured him.

Tannis barely stirred when he wrapped her in a blanket and carried her out to the car. He didn't bother with seat belts, but held her slumped against his shoulder for the short drive to the clinic. Once inside, he hovered anxiously while Dr. Ellis examined Tannis. She roused enough to talk to him briefly, but the minute he was finished she sank back into a restless doze.

"What's wrong with her?" Tom blurred. "Does she need to be hospitalized?"

"No hospital." Tannis's eyes opened and she frowned at Tom.

"You'll go if the doctor says you need to," Tom snapped back.

"No," she croaked. "Please...can't afford the time." She waved a hand at the doctor. "No hospital."

Tom sighed. "She's been trying to work two jobs to pay for her mother's care in a nursing home." Then he looked squarely at the doctor. "But if you think she needs to be hospitalized, she will be."

The doctor looked thoughtful. "She's certainly a sick lady right now. Is there anyone who could stay with her and look after her for a few days?"

"I can." Tom ignored Tannis's frantic head-shaking.

"She has what we often refer to as 'walking pneumonia,' and it's exacerbated by exhaustion," the doctor informed him. "No doubt about it, she's going to have to take it easy for a while. No more working two jobs. But with proper medication, diet and plenty of rest, she should be fine." He turned to the wall of cabinets in the small examining room. "I'm going to give her something to bring that fever down. I'll write a prescription for you to fill first thing in the morning. She should take all of it, even after she feels better. Try to get a lot of liquids into her. If after twenty-four hours, she appears to be feeling worse or isn't responding to the medication, call me immediately. She might have to be admitted, after all."

Getting her home was easy. She fell into a deep sleep and didn't stir at all when he carried her into the house and up to her room again. Before he laid her down, he maneuvered the sheets and blankets back to the foot of the bed on the side nearest the door.

Sitting on the side of the bed, he untied her white work shoes and set them aside. He watched her for a moment, snuggled in the big blanket he'd wrapped around her for the trip to the clinic.

He sighed. When he'd overheard her explaining to Amy that she had to be careful about her clothing as she got older, not to be deliberately provocative, he'd suffered an enormous pang of guilt for the way he'd been spying on Tannis's private time in her hot tub. The feeling returned now as he contemplated undressing her. Sure, he could leave her in her clothing all night, but she'd probably be uncomfortable—oh, what the hell. He might as well admit it. He was going to remove her clothing, but not only because he was worried about her comfort.

Because he was base enough to enjoy the thought of baring her body to his gaze, even when she wasn't awake enough to know it.

Thinking ahead, he went to her dresser and dug through the drawers until he found a frothy gown to put on her. Then, slowly, he unbuttoned her jumper and her blouse and pulled them off. Her half-slip came next. By the time he rolled her panty hose down her legs his fingers were shaking and he could feel the sweat rolling down his back.

He drank in the sight of her body clad only in panties and bra, critically noting that she'd lost even more weight than he'd first thought. She was so sick! Panic and anger fought for a hold on his mind, distracting him momentarily. She'd refused his help with a loan and look at her now. All he'd wanted to do was to make things easier for her.

As he had for Mary.

But there was a difference here. Tannis wasn't going to die. He could see to that. Glancing back down at her, his gaze was drawn to her nearly bare breasts. Through the lacy bra, he could just see the darker outline of her nipples. His breath caught in his chest, and abruptly, he realized that he couldn't do this any longer. It wasn't fair to Tannis and besides, he was making himself crazy.

Bunching up the gown, he slipped it over her head and pulled it down over her torso before sliding his hands beneath her and unhooking her bra. Without hesitation, he pulled the bra away, stuffed her arms through the ribbon straps of the gown and pulled it quickly down to cover her. Just as quickly, he straightened her limbs into a more comfortable-looking position and covered her with all the sheets and blankets on the bed.

She woke in the middle of the night, thirsty and disoriented. When she turned her head to look at the clock, the room spun alarmingly and she groaned. Almost instantly, her bedside lamp was switched on and a voice said, "It's all right, Tannis."

She automatically flung up a hand to protect her eyes from the too-sudden brightness, but she'd recognize Tom's voice anywhere.

"What are you doing in my bedroom in the middle of the night?" Though it was a demand for information, it came out as a fractured whisper.

"Keeping an eye on you. Want a drink?"

She nodded. Cautiously she removed her hand from her eyes, squinting in the light. Large fingers held a glass of ice water in front of her, but when she tried to sit up the room whirled before her again and a frightening weakness assailed her muscles. Now she understood what the phrase, "weak as a kitten," meant.

As if he knew without being told how she felt, Tom wedged a broad arm behind her back and slowly levered her into a more or less vertical position. Sick as she was, she was acutely aware of his nearness as he rested her back against his chest and guided the glass to her mouth. She drank greedily, enjoying the feel of the cool liquid on her swollen throat.

Finally Tom took the glass away. As he lay her back against the pillows, she stiffened in shock, realizing for the first time that she was wearing a lacy nightgown. She hadn't worn this particular nightgown in years, preferring oversize T-shirts to the pretty lingerie that her ex-husband had liked. "What...? Where...?" she whispered, hastily covering herself with the sheet.

Again, Tom understood. He shifted his body to pull the bed covers out from beneath him where he sat facing her on the edge of the bed. "After we got back from the clinic, I put you in nightclothes. I thought you'd be more comfortable."

"Clinic?" She thought back, but everything after that awful scene at the restaurant was a blank. And he'd said...that meant he'd undressed her...? She couldn't handle that line of thought so she switched to another piece of the puzzle. "Did I see a doctor?"

"Dr. Ellis. Don't you remember coming home from work?"

She shook her head, finally giving up in frustration. "How?"

"You drove." Tom's mouth compressed. "Without lights. I glanced out my office window just in time to see you pull into your driveway, get out of the car and fall flat."

Oh, Lord. She could tell from the agonized memories flaring in his eyes what he'd thought...after Mary. Stretching out a tentative hand, she touched his knee. "I'm sorry."

"I know." Tom's big, warm hand closed over hers.

Another thought teased at the edges of her mind, gradually coming into focus. "You can go home now. I'll be all right."

His mouth hardened into a straight line. "In case the fact has eluded you, you're a very sick woman right now. Dr. Ellis met us at the clinic and looked you over. I'm staying for a while because you can't take care of yourself."

"What about Jebbie and—"

"I got a baby-sitter, and she'll be with the kids all night."

"You don't have to stay," she whispered. Her throat hurt and keeping her eyes open was becoming a major effort.

Tom turned his hand over and roughly took hers, shoving it back under the covers and switching off the light. "Go to sleep, Tannis. You're fighting pneumonia and I promised the doctor I'd stay with you." His tone grew sarcastic. "If this is an example of the way you take care of yourself, I'd hate to see you let yourself go."

She took exception to his nastiness. "I don't…need you." But the clouds were closing in and she couldn't remember the rest of what she wanted to pound into his head.…

Four

Two more times during the night she roused and he got her to drink a little bit. She was quiet and he didn't think she realized who he was or where she was. But as he lay her back on the pillow just after seven in the morning, she suddenly grabbed his forearm in a surprisingly strong grip.

"My uniform...have to take it back today. Lew won't let me have my paycheck unless I hand in my uniform. Have to give back the uniform—"

"I'll take care of it," he said, more to soothe her than because he really meant it.

But she didn't relax. "I have to deposit the check," she mumbled. "Need to pay the mortgage this week...."

"I promise I'll handle everything," he said. "We'll talk more about it in the morning." She sounded so frantic. Just how desperate was her situation? He'd known she was worrying about money, from things the kids had said and the way she'd turned down his baby-sitting offer, but she sounded as if she were genuinely worried about making ends meet.

"You can't fix everything." Her grip on his arm suddenly relaxed. In horror, he saw tears well up in her expressive eyes and begin to trail back into her hair. Then her eyes began to drift closed.

"Tannis!" He shook her arm roughly, startling her awake again. "What's happened? Why are you crying?"

Misery filled her gaze. "Oh, Tom," she whispered. "I got fired. I was late to work and Lew was so angry." The tears increased again, soaking the auburn curls at her temples. "I begged him to give me a second chance, I told him I was sick...but he fired me. What am I going to do?"

Rage rose within him at the callousness of the manager. Anyone could see Tannis was trustworthy. Didn't the man allow for a mistake? He stepped hard on the impulse to run out of the room and drive to the guy's house and throttle him. Instead, he carefully wiped away her tears with his fingers. "We'll figure out something when you're feeling better. Come on, honey, close your eyes and relax. It'll all be okay."

It was a weak promise, but to his surprise, it worked. She drifted back into deeper sleep as he sat turning his thoughts around in his mind. Finally he realized this was probably as good a time as any to run next door and check on his own family before Tannis roused again.

Antha, the baby-sitter, had everything under control, just as he'd expected. He'd been in touch with her by phone already this morning and she'd even made lunches for the kids.

Jeb met him before he'd even gotten in the front door. "Antha says Tannis is sick and you have to take care of her." His little face was puckered with anxiety.

Tom heard the fear that lurked behind his son's words, and it tore at his heart. No six-year-old should have to worry that the people around him were going to die. His throat tight, he went down on one knee to grip Jeb's shoulders reassuringly. "Tannis is going to get better. I'll let you visit her in a day or two and you can see for yourself how she's doing."

Thinking of Tannis and how ill she'd been last night jogged his memory. He had to let someone from her school know. He figured the best place to start was with the principal, whom he knew from the community adult basketball league in which he'd played before Mary died.

Looking up the number, he hoped Harry Tenlow would forgive him for the early call.

"Hello?"

"Harry, it's Tom Hayes."

"Howdy, Tom. Haven't seen you in way too long." There was an awkward pause as Harry remembered just why he hadn't seen much of Tom lately.

"Longer than I'd like." Tom was used to people not knowing quite what to say to him. "Basketball doesn't fit into my schedule anymore, much as I wish it did. But I have another reason for calling you this morning."

"What's up?"

"Tannis Carlson is sick. I need to know who to contact to get a substitute for her classes for today and probably for at least a week."

"You called the right person. I handle all substitute needs within my school. Each principal in Albemarle County is responsible for his own school." Harry had switched effortlessly into a professional mode. Then his voice warmed with concern. "What happened to Tannis?"

Tom gave him a condensed version of her illness, finishing with, "She has pneumonia and the doctor says she's going to need to be very careful not to do too much too soon."

Harry snorted. "The doctor obviously doesn't know our Mrs. Carlson very well." Then he sobered. "Tannis is one of my best teachers. And she never misses school, so she has plenty of sick leave. She'll have to have a doctor's verification for an extended absence, but the time off is no problem. Also, it would be helpful if she could talk to the substitute teacher sometime next week if she's able."

"She had a bunch of papers in her book bag," Tom said, dismissing the details of how he'd opened her bag and frankly snooped. "Are any of them important?"

Harry waved that aside. "We'll limp along today. Why don't I call you Sunday afternoon? If she's well enough to give a few instructions, I can relay them to the substitute then."

"Thanks, Harry."

"No trouble." Open curiosity colored the principal's voice. "Are you taking care of Tannis?"

"For the time being." Tom didn't rise to the interest in Harry's question. "She doesn't take too well to being nursed."

Harry laughed. "I just bet." But his next comment was serious. "Tannis is a fine woman. If I wasn't happily married . . . You could do worse, Hayes. A lot worse."

Tom was startled. Was Harry suggesting he marry Tannis? Aloud, he said mildly, "I'm just helping her out, Harry. She's been a good friend."

"If you say so." There was a smile in Harry's voice. "Tell Tannis to get better and not to worry—I'll take care of things at this end."

"Thanks." Tom hung up the phone absently.

After he'd called his secretary to arrange for her to pick up Tannis's prescription, take her uniform back to the restaurant and bring some of his work over to the house, he couldn't stop thinking about what Harry had said.

When Tannis awoke again, it was full daylight. A shaft of weak winter sunshine fell through the partially open miniblinds to make bars of brightness across her knees. She lay perfectly still as memory seeped back.

How much was dream, how much reality?

She definitely remembered the ugly scene at the restaurant. Then, nothing . . . maybe a hazy half remembrance of Dr. Ellis saying something about the hospital . . . but nothing concrete until she'd awoken and Tom had switched on the bedside light that had so hurt her eyes.

Oh, God, if only it had been a dream. She'd lost her evening job. And she knew with dead certainty, from the hollowed-out, shaky way she felt, that it would be a long time before she could take on another one.

So the decision had been made for her, in a sense. Funny how her options seemed so clear now. One possibility would be to move back home to Culpeper. Get an apartment in the little town where the prices were nothing like the sky-high rates in Charlottesville and bring her mother to live with her if she could find a suitable apartment. If she was lucky enough to get another teaching job midyear, she might manage to pay for a caregiver to look after her mother during the day. Night duty would be her job, but it wouldn't cost anything.

On the whole, Plan One stank. Her mother would be stressed and upset if she was moved again. And what was more, Tannis's life would be a living hell. Wearily she thought of all the occasions over the past few years when her mother had defended Jeremy. Mama knew exactly who was to blame for the breakup of Tannis and Jeremy's marriage... and it wasn't Jeremy.

Plan One might work, but it would be at the cost of Tannis's sanity.

Okay, so there had to be other choices. She worked around every angle she could think of that would allow her to stay in Charlottesville and keep her home in Forest Lakes. But that didn't take long.

Familiar ground. She'd gone in those same circles for days already. There was no way to make that combination work.

You're going to have to sell the house.

She sighed, feeling the dead weight of despair settle over her like a shroud. There was no way around it. The house was going to have to go. If she got an apartment somewhere close with a roommate, she might be able to pay for Mama's care and her own living expenses without exhausting all her funds. The residue from the sale she could invest to cover rainy days.

And there would be plenty of those, she decided. But on the whole, Plan Two got her vote. It had one thing going for it that Tannis couldn't dispute. Her mother wouldn't have to be moved, and Tannis wouldn't have to endure Mama's scathing opinions of her only child's failures as a wife on a daily basis.

Her old counselor would have cheered, Tannis reflected dismally. She would say that Tannis was taking charge of her life and refusing to let life's problems conquer her. So why did it feel as if she'd lost?

She sighed again, then sat up with cautious movements. At least the room didn't spin this morning, although she still felt horribly weak. As she donned the robe that lay across the foot of the bed and made a beeline for the bathroom, she thought of Tom.

Calling the doctor, staying all night and nursing her . . . no question about it, he'd certainly discharged any obligations he thought he owed her for her help during Mary's illness. The memory of him admitting he'd undressed her rose to taunt her and she felt her cheeks burning. How could she ever face him again?

Speaking of facing him, she wondered where he'd gone. Every time she'd woken during the night he'd been right there, encouraging her to drink and to rest again. She assumed he'd gone home, or more likely, to work...work! Jarred out of the lethargy that weighed on her, she rushed back to the bedside to look at the clock: 10:37.

Oh, no. *Please,* no. A horrible feeling of déjà vu assailed her. This couldn't happen two days in a row, could it? Would she lose her teaching job—

"What are you doing out of bed?" Tom's voice had the daunting timbre of a rather irritated drill sergeant. He stood near the foot of the bed with his hands on his hips, eyeing her as if he was planning to put her back in it forcibly. Even dressed in casual clothes and unshaven, he exuded raw power.

Automatically she began to scurry back under the covers. Then she realized what she was doing. Forcing herself not to back down from the steely disapproval in his emerald eyes, she gathered the remnants of her tattered dignity around her. "I'm planning on dressing and going to work, for which I'm already late. Why didn't you set my alarm?" Unfortunately she'd forgotten the scratchy quality of her voice. It ruined the haughty tone.

He completely ignored the question anyway. "Harry got a sub for you. She'll teach your class until at least the end of next week."

"Mr. Tenlow got a...how did he know?" Her throat hurt. She sank onto the bed. This was too much. Since last night, her whole world seemed to have been turned inside out and upside down.

Tom came and stood in front of her. When he cupped her cheek in his palm with easy familiarity, she pulled away in alarm. "What are you doing?"

"Checking to see if you have a fever." He replaced his hand calmly. "Why don't you get back in bed?

You're still a little warm, but nothing like last evening." He turned and picked up a glass of water and two pills from the bedside table. When he turned back and fixed her with an unblinking stare, her defiance wilted and she complied, crawling under the covers before her legs gave out on her.

Then he sat beside her and offered her the medication. "Here. My secretary, Polly, had your prescriptions filled this morning. The sooner we get you started on these, the sooner you'll be feeling like yourself again."

She glared at him, trying her best to ignore the shivers of sensation that quivered through her at the feel of his muscled thigh firmly pressing against her. "What's this 'we' stuff? I'm the one who's sick. I'm the one who lost one job and could lose another if I don't get back to school. I'm the one who—wait a minute, who paid for those prescriptions?"

"I did. You can pay me back. I also had Polly return your uniform for you and pick up your check. If you tell me where you bank, I'll deposit it for you."

His gentleness was almost her undoing. Rigidly, her gaze followed a slightly off-color piece of thread in the blanket that covered her bed. She swallowed hard without taking her eyes off the thread and winced when her throat protested. "I—thank you, Tom. I appreciate your help and I'm sorry if I seem ungrateful." Meekly she took the proffered medication from him and downed both pills with one swallow of water.

"You've been under a lot of stress," he said. Then he lifted a finger to her chin and tilted her face up to his. "Why didn't you tell me how bad your financial situation was?"

She gazed at him mutely. What was she supposed to say? "It wasn't your problem," she whispered.

"Last night you told me you lost your job at the restaurant. What will you do now?"

She shrugged, dropping her gaze to stare blindly at the pattern in his cream cotton sweater.

His breath hissed out explosively. "You must see you can't continue to push yourself like this. What if you'd hit someone driving in that condition last night? Or driven off the road? With no headlights, it could have been hours before anyone found you. What if I hadn't seen you fall and you'd lain out there all night?"

"I'm going to sell the house."

Silence.

Finally she glanced at Tom. "Did you hear me? I'm going to sell the house and look for a roommate who will share an apartment with me."

Saying it aloud didn't make her feel any better, any more resigned. In fact, it made her want to scream and cry. She gritted her teeth. "It's the only way."

Tom came to life then. His hand clenched into a fist, then just as suddenly opened, palm down on his knee. "It's not your only option," he said quietly.

Puzzled, she shifted to face him where he sat on the edge of her bed. "I've been thinking it through, Tom, and I really don't have—"

"You could marry me."

Marry him?

Tom's eyes were pure silver, without a hint of their

usual green, so intense that she'd swear they would reflect her image like twin mirrors if she got close enough to look. Tannis swallowed. She couldn't break contact with those eyes. Surely he hadn't said...could he *really* have said what she thought she'd heard?

Her voice was no more than a whisper. "I could...*marry* you?"

Tom nodded, still holding her gaze. Other than that one curt movement of his head, he could have been made of marble, so still was he holding himself.

She offered him what she knew was at best a weak smile. "You must be getting sick, too. Are you running a fever?"

Not a hint of an answering smile touched his lips. "I feel fine. Tannis, listen to me before you say anything."

"Tom, I can't—"

"Shhh." He covered her mouth with his palm. "Just listen."

As before when he'd touched her so casually, the intimacy of the move startled her and sent a sizzling heat down to center in her belly. Uncertainly she nodded.

He removed his hand from her mouth and stood, pacing to the far end of the room and pivoting to face her. The move reminded her of his occupation. Although she knew he rarely had cause to try a case in court, she would be stupid to forget about Tom's steel-trap mind. He could probably have her agreeing to commit herself to an asylum if he really tried.

A wave of weariness swept over her. Despite her shock at his words, all she really wanted to do was lie down and sleep. But she forced herself to focus on what he was saying.

"Marriage would be good for both of us." Tom speared her with his gaze again. "We wouldn't be going into it with any silly illusions about love. We both have needs, problems that marriage could solve."

He came a step closer, watching her in a way that reminded her of a hawk when it caught sight of a mouse too far from its nest. "My children need a mother. Amy in particular needs a woman's attention. Both she and Jeb already love you so there wouldn't be quite the period of adjustment there might be with a total stranger."

Beneath her lacy gown, Tannis's heart gave a painful tug at the idea of Tom marrying someone else. The thought had never occurred to her before—or maybe she hadn't allowed it to surface—but she found it a distinctly unpleasant one.

Tom was still talking. "I'm not interested in having my wife act as a housekeeper. I want someone who will devote herself to making a family for me and the kids. Someone I can share the parenting with. If you marry me, you can continue to teach if that's what you want. I'll hire a housekeeper or someone to clean. You could use your salary any way you like." He came a step closer and sat on the edge of the bed. "You'd have plenty of money for your mother's care."

His words assaulted her weakened defenses, and dimly Tannis understood that that was exactly what he wanted, to catch her with her guard down. She should have resented the idea, but his words wove soft, cozy pictures of a family—her very own family—in her mind and she found herself relaxing, drifting with the images.

Then he took her hands in his larger ones and she was yanked back to awareness. His voice was low as he said, "There's something else I should tell you. I don't know how you feel about children, but I'd be happy if you wanted to have a baby of your own. I've always wanted a large family."

A baby of your own. He knew just how deep to plunge the knife—

Then Tom raised her hands and pressed the backs of her fingers to his lips and her gaze flew to his face. His eyelids drooped, but beneath the lowered lids she could see a fierce, hot light burning in his eyes that shortened her breath and gave her odd sensations deep in her abdomen, as if tiny gymnasts were practicing their routines in her womb.

"Tannis…" His voice had dropped a full octave and was little more than a growl. His hot breath blasted the tender skin at the back of her hands where he held them. "We're good together, you and I. The sex between us will be great. It's one of the things I miss most about marriage. I'd be a faithful husband."

He leaned toward her and she closed her eyes helplessly. Even if she hadn't been so sick, her limbs were too weak to allow her to move away from him. One large palm slid up underneath her hair and cradled her cheek. "Look at me," he whispered, and she opened her eyes to see his face filling her vision only inches away, his mobile lips moving enticingly. "Just rest now, and think about what I've said. We'll talk later, when you're feeling better." Then his lips brushed along her cheekbone and feathered over her mouth before he pushed himself off the bed and pulled the covers up around her.

"Sleep now," he said, and the warm, tender note in his voice was gone and he was Tom again, the stern, unsmiling man who made her heart beat faster with his mere presence. "I'll check on you at lunchtime."

At noon, he made some chicken soup and fed it to her himself. Tannis protested at first, but when he made it clear she wasn't getting out of bed for at least another full day, she gave in with less of a fight than he'd expected.

Seeing Tannis propped up against her pillows, docilely opening her mouth for the spoon, her dark red hair emphasizing the porcelain color of her skin, Tom's gut clenched as he realized anew how ill she'd been. The Tannis Carlson he knew was a prickly, feisty lady who could take anything life dished out. He'd have gotten his finger bitten off if he'd tried to feed her by hand a few days ago.

She'd eaten less than half the soup when she placed her hand on his wrist as he returned the spoon to the bowl. "No more. Please."

Tom looked down at her small hand lying warm against his skin. He knew she wasn't really delicate and helpless but she aroused in him protective instincts that he'd thought were dead and buried. Not to mention some other less chivalrous instincts as well. He eyed the lace that softened the low neckline of her gown, remembering the smooth, silky skin beneath it with a fascination that bordered on obsession.

His thoughts were leading to trouble. As badly as he might want her, there was no way Tannis was well

enough to indulge in some afternoon delight right
now. Reluctantly he pulled his gaze back to her face,
realizing she was still waiting for an answer. "Okay,"
he said. "But you have to promise me you'll eat some
for an afternoon snack later."

She smiled at him and raised her right hand. "I
promise." Then her face sobered. "Tom, I've been
thinking about what you said—"

Alarm bells rang in his mind. *She was going to refuse to marry him!* Quickly he said, "I have to get
back to work now. It can wait awhile." He stood and
picked up the soup bowl, pulling her blankets into
place in a gesture that was becoming second nature
before he strode from the room.

Amy was a willing nurse when he explained what he
wanted her to do, and after school she took a snack
over to Tannis. At suppertime, a friend of hers from
school came by and offered to stay for a few hours,
which suited him just fine.

He thought he'd put forth plenty of logical reasons
why marriage between them would be a good move.
Apparently she hadn't been convinced. He had to figure out a way to talk her into marrying him.

She slept soundly all through Friday night. Tom had
come over briefly just before bedtime but he hadn't
stayed. He'd been acting strangely ever since he had
proposed marriage yesterday morning.

Maybe he was having second thoughts and he didn't
know how to get out of it gracefully.

She didn't know if that would be a relief or a disappointment to her. She'd been totally, completely
shocked to pieces when he'd first asked her to marry

him. It was a crazy idea and she was crazy even to consider it. But as he'd talked, and in the long hours she'd had to think about marrying Tom, she had to admit that it was a sound idea.

He was right. It would be a perfect solution to her financial problems. But she couldn't take advantage of him that way. Even contemplating the idea made her feel like a money-grubbing witch.

On the other hand, would it be taking advantage? She'd seen the stress Tom was under trying to maintain a household and be both mother and father to his children. She might not be the world's greatest housekeeper, but she was pretty sure she could make Tom's life easier and she already loved Jeb and Amy.

And Tom had assured her he didn't want a housekeeper. So the shortcomings that Jeremy had so despised wouldn't be an issue in this marriage. She'd be going into this one with her eyes wide open. *Knowing* Tom didn't love her would help. And she wasn't about to allow her heart to weave any foolish fantasies where he was concerned. That way no one could be disappointed and they'd both know where they stood.

She had the added advantage of having seen Tom with Mary in his first marriage. He'd always treated Mary with consideration and respect. But, when it came right down to the clinch, the most important thing Tom had said yesterday had been his words about a child of her own. Never having the chance to become a mother had been one of the most difficult issues she'd had to face after her divorce. She'd always desperately wanted a baby. Tom couldn't have known that, and yet he'd zeroed in on the weakest link in her defenses...that link that ultimately made all of her hemming and hawing pointless.

After thinking about marriage to Tom Hayes for a day and a half now, she'd decided to do it. If Tom still wanted to marry her—which was by no means a certainty—she was going to accept his offer and do her very best to make his family happy.

The one unknown in her plan was the physical aspect of their marriage. Tom had made it very clear that if she married him, it would be a real marriage in every sense of the word. Thinking of sharing a bed, sharing intimacies with Tom made her stomach quiver. But what if she disappointed him? Jeremy had rarely made her feel more than mild arousal, had never once made her feel the flutters of excitement that assailed her nerve endings at Tom's slightest touch. If her response to Tom's caresses to date were significant, she shouldn't be worrying—when he kissed her she felt like a brush fire receiving a dousing with kerosene! Still, the thought of all that marriage implied made her nervous.

But along with the nerves crept an insatiable, insidious curiosity that undermined any second thoughts.

So she'd decided to accept his offer.

If he hadn't changed his mind.

Saturday slipped past and Tannis began to feel well enough to move about her house. Tom wouldn't let her lift a finger, not even to load the dishwasher. By Sunday she was beginning to feel guilty about her enforced slothdom, even though the mere act of walking down the stairs was enough to tire her.

That evening, Tom came over about six o'clock, bearing a loaded basket from which delicious smells were emanating.

"Lasagna and Italian bread, with salad and cherry cobbler for dessert," he elaborated when she lifted a corner of the basket's covering and peeked.

She shook her head in wonder. "You've become quite a chef. I'll get fat if I let you feed me much longer."

Tom surveyed her figure. "Good. You need to eat until you get your curves back."

"Tom!" Startled by the frank assessment, she felt her cheeks warming as she recalled exactly how he knew about her body. "I don't want my curves back. I wouldn't have chosen this method of weight loss, but I'm pleased with the result."

"I liked your curves," he told her simply. He came around the corner of the bar and placed a heaping plate of food at her place. "Now eat."

Tannis began to obey without thinking. Then, halfway into her chair, she stopped and stood again. Behind her, Tom said, "What's the matter?"

"I want you to stay until I'm done." She turned and poked a finger into his chest. "And then I want to talk about what you said the other day."

He didn't pretend to misunderstand. "Okay. I wanted you feeling better before you made your decision." He seized her hand in his and pulled it away from his chest, kissing the tip of her finger and flashing her his rare grin. "I knew when you started to act touchy and independent again you were recovering."

Tannis stared at him for a minute. That smile zapped every brain cell she had into immobility. She would have loved to toss back a snappy comment, but her mind wasn't functioning properly. It kept replaying a mental film of Tom with that devilish grin on his face, kissing her hand. Finally she flounced into her seat and attacked the meal he'd prepared.

Amy came in while she was savoring the last bites of the cobbler. The girl tossed a large envelope on the counter with an apologetic smile. "I almost forgot to give you this. It's from your class. I brought it home from school on Friday, but I just found it in my book bag when I went to get out my homework tonight."

From Tannis's kitchen, Tom directed a stern look at his daughter. "You told me you didn't have any homework."

"I just forgot," Amy said. A defensive tone crept into her voice. "Besides, it's only a few math problems. No big deal."

"Not to you, perhaps, but it's important to me that you keep up with your schoolwork. If you haven't finished your math, please say good-night to Tannis and get to work."

Amy's face fell. "G'night," she mumbled.

Tannis caught her hand as she passed. "Thank you for helping take care of me this weekend, Amy. I don't know what I'd have done without good friends like you and your dad."

The stiff set of the girl's shoulders relaxed. "You're welcome. I'm glad you're getting better." She sighed. "Guess I better get started on the math. See you tomorrow."

"Be sure to come visit me after school," Tannis said.

"Sure thing." The twelve-year-old turned and headed out the front door.

Tannis opened the envelope while Tom cleared her dishes away. The substitute had had Tannis's fourth-grade class make cards for her. As Tannis read her students' messages, tears welled in her eyes.

"Hey, what's this?" Tom slung a dish towel on the bar and came around to cup her chin in his hand. "Why the tears?"

Tannis sniffed. "Just feeling sorry for myself." She got up and accompanied him into her living room and they settled on the couch side by side. "I hate the thought of losing a whole week of teaching time. I only have these children for one hundred and eighty days, and we only get about five good hours of instructional time in each day—it's not nearly enough to teach them everything I want them to know before they move into fifth grade!"

Tom took her hand in a loose clasp, rubbing his thumb back and forth across her knuckles. "Teaching means a lot to you, doesn't it?"

She nodded. "Young minds are very special . . . and very vulnerable. I think it's vitally important to challenge students intellectually while still giving them the limits and support they need."

"That's easier said than done," Tom said ruefully. "As I've discovered from painful experience." Then his gaze fell to their linked hands. "Tannis, have you had enough time to consider my proposal?"

Aware that her whole future hinged on what was about to pass between them, Tannis nodded slowly. "I have. Does your offer still stand?"

A strange expression crossed Tom's face. "Of course."

"I thought you'd changed your mind and were hoping I'd decline."

"I want you to be my wife." For once Tom's intense eye contact was absent. A muscle ticked in his jaw as he continued to stare at their joined hands and she became aware of how tightly he was gripping her fingers. "Will you marry me or not?"

"I've considered everything you said," she told him, "and I'd be honored to marry you. I promise to do everything I can to make your family happy."

Tom dropped her hand and turned to face her, gazing into her eyes. "And I promise to take care of you." He reached into the pocket of his trousers and pulled out a small box, giving her a crooked smile as he placed the box in her hands. "I felt optimistic."

"Oh..." Tannis was speechless. This was basically a business arrangement between them; she'd never expected Tom to present her with a ring. Her hands shook as she opened the box and her mouth formed a silent *O* of wonder as a sparkling diamond in an antique gold filigree setting was revealed. "This is the loveliest ring I've ever seen."

Tom reached for the box and extracted the ring. "It was my grandmother's. Mary wanted a new ring, so she never wore it. If you'd prefer something contemporary, you don't have to wear it."

Tannis shook her head, fighting to speak past the lump in her throat. "Don't you dare talk about another ring. I want this one!"

Five

Tom smiled as he gently picked up her left hand and slid the ring onto her third finger. "It's yours. Welcome to the Hayes family."

A tear rolled down her cheek and Tannis fought not to dissolve completely. "Thank you for making this special. You didn't have to, you know."

"Of course I did," he told her, slipping one hand beneath her legs and the other around her back and lifting her into his lap. "You're a very special lady. And I'm very lucky you've agreed to be my wife."

As she linked her arms around his neck, he lowered his head and sought her lips. Tannis never thought of refusing, kissing him back with all the passion he aroused in her, opening her mouth for the gentle intrusion of his tongue as her hands traced the shape of his muscled back. He was hard and hot, all man, and

she was aware of him as she'd never been of Jeremy in
their brief years together. When his hand slipped from
her waist up to trace feather strokes of sensation
around the fullness of her breast, she sighed into his
mouth.

The part of her brain that hadn't short-circuited at
his touch sternly reminded her that sex wasn't love.
Don't confuse the two, she admonished herself... and then she forgot to think at all.

He kept up the gentle stimulation, never actually
touching the crest of her breast, and Tannis began to
shift impatiently on his lap as arrows of tension drew
her nipples into tight beads of need. Why didn't he
touch her there? He kept up a rhythmic assault on her
mouth, stoking the rising fire inside her until she
grasped his wrist in frustration and placed his hand
fully on the mound of one breast.

He responded immediately, rotating his flattened
fingers over the taut tip until her nipple stood out
clearly against the fleece fabric of the soft sweat suit
she wore. When he transferred his attention to the
other breast, she whimpered into his mouth, and he
gave a low growl of satisfaction.

"You like that, don't you?" His hand deftly dipped
beneath the ribbed hem of her shirt, flipping up the
covering of her bra to find bare skin. "Isn't that better?" he said against her mouth as his fingers shaped
and twisted the swollen tip.

"Yes, yes." It was a whisper as she twisted her head
restlessly against his shoulder and her fingers dug into
the thickness of his dark hair.

Tom bent over her, and she felt the heat of his
breath against her skin an instant before her nipple

was surrounded by the slick, hot suction of his lips and tongue working, suckling with steady pressure.

Tannis nearly jumped out of her skin at the intensity of the new sensation. Automatically she lifted her sweatshirt out of the way to give him better access. Tom chuckled deep in his throat. Against her thigh, she could feel him shifting, sliding and shifting again, rubbing himself against her as he worked her breast. His free hand stroked down her torso over her bare flesh until her waistband halted him. Almost absently, the finger traveled back and forth along the elasticized fabric for long moments. She was so engrossed in the more demanding sensations his mouth was creating at her breast that when his finger slipped beneath the waistband and dipped beneath her panties to discover the feminine mound beneath that she didn't protest, indeed, she barely noticed.

And then, with a suddenness that wrung a surprised cry from her, she *did* notice. One steadily encroaching finger slid between her thighs, down through the soft curls between her legs to the even softer flesh beneath. Her hips jerked, and she felt a powerful need to rub herself against that hot, hard finger. She felt a rush of moisture dampen her, and she hid her face against Tom's shoulder in embarrassment as she realized he certainly could feel it, too.

He lifted his head, and to her mortification, inspected her flushed face. "Don't be shy," he said, and his voice was deep and rough and incredibly sexy. "You're so soft and wet... do you want me, Tannis?"

His finger was doing erotic things, creating sensations she hadn't even known she could feel, and she moaned. "I just want to make you happy," she managed to say.

Tom smiled, but it was more of a strained baring of teeth. "Oh, you're making me happy, baby. In fact," he went on as he slowly began to withdraw his hand from its intimate cocoon, "You're making me feel *too* good."

"How can you feel too good?"

He sucked in his breath as she squirmed against him so she could see his face better. "You know what I mean."

"No." Tannis took a deep breath, passion suddenly derailed. "I don't think I do. My past sexual experience was confined to five-minute experiences in a dark bedroom. I can't say it ever felt *good*." She swallowed. "I don't want to disappoint you."

At her words, he'd gone very still. Briefly his features hardened, and she wondered at the look of anger that disappeared before she could be absolutely certain she'd seen it. Withdrawing his hand completely, he took his time about pulling her clothes into place, finally resting his big, warm hand on her abdomen and her heart sank. Had he stopped because of what she'd said?

"You won't disappoint me," he told her with finality. He calmly laid his hand over her left breast, just below her heart. "There's passion in here, and together we're going to tap it."

Reassured by his words, if not convinced, Tannis laid her hand over his. "You didn't have to stop."

"Yes, I did. I promised myself we'd wait until the wedding, and I'm in real danger of breaking my promise."

"But it's okay if you want to... if we want to..."

"I want to," Tom responded, dropping a lingering kiss on her lips that turned into something that left them both breathing heavily when he finally tore himself away. "But we're going to wait until after the wedding. When we make love for the first time, I want to have all night to savor this beautiful body and to teach you how good we're going to be. And I don't want to have to worry about protection. If you get pregnant, no one's going to count backward on their fingers to see if a child of ours is legitimate."

He was so blunt! She blushed, unaccountably embarrassed at his talk of pregnancy. The idea of Tom's baby growing in her body was still an abstract she couldn't grasp. "I'd like to get pregnant right away," she confessed.

Tom pressed a short, stinging kiss onto her lips. "First, we've got to get married. How does two weeks from Saturday sound?"

"Two weeks from Saturday? Are you crazy? We can't possibly get married that fast."

Tom laughed at her panicked expression. "Sure we can. All we need is a license and a minister."

He was right. This was a second marriage for each of them, nothing more than a marriage of convenience. The trappings of a large, formal wedding were unnecessary. They wouldn't need any attendants except the children. Still...

"But what about this house? Will we sell it? I'll have to go through my things and decide what we want to keep."

"We'll work on it together." Tom's voice had a decisive ring. "I'll call a realtor tomorrow to come and give us an appraisal and get it on the market."

It made sense. Why wait? But she'd never been an impulsive person. "It seems like we're rushing it," she hedged. "What about Amy and Jeb? Will that give them enough time to adjust?"

"I suspect they'll be as anxious as I am to make you legal. Besides, the sooner you sell this house, the better you'll feel about your finances."

She couldn't argue with that logic, either. He made her feel like she was swimming the wrong way against a powerful current. With a sigh, she relaxed against him again. "All right. Two weeks from Saturday it is."

The first week passed in a blur. The realtor had three people interested in her house by the following Friday, before it even went on the market officially. Tom wouldn't let her do any packing, since she was still convalescing, but she made list after list. Every evening, Tom, Amy and Jeb came over and she directed them as to what would be taken next door and what would be packed up to be sold.

Jeb had taken the news of his father's impending nuptials with equanimity. "Neat," he said. "Will you come to my ball games like the other mothers?"

"Of course I will, Jeb," Tannis promised him, touched by the simple request. She didn't miss the grimace of pain that twisted Tom's features for a moment. "I'll yell every time you come up to bat, too."

After Jeb had gone to bed, Tom said. "He never said a word to me about not having a mother at the games."

"His world is still very concrete," Tannis responded gently. "Not having a mom makes Jeb different and kids mind being different. You're marrying me to change that." Hearing the words spoken aloud squeezed her heart in some small, indefinable way, but she ignored it and forced herself to act naturally with Tom. He'd made no secret of why he wanted her as his wife. She should be content—she was getting a bargain, getting all the things for which she'd longed without ever having to risk her heart again. That was exactly what she wanted.

Wasn't it?

Jeb might have been accepting, but Amy had a few pointed questions that she voiced one evening while Tom and Jebbie were busy carting a load of books over to the Hayes's house.

"Tannis..."

From the wary note in Amy's voice, Tannis could tell she was going to get her first lesson in dealing with the convoluted thought process of an adolescent.

"Will I have to call you 'Mom' now?" Also for the first time, Tannis could read a hint of defiance directed at her.

"No, Amy, not unless that's what you choose to call me," she said calmly, continuing to pack up more books. "You can keep calling me Tannis if you're comfortable with that. You had a mother whom you loved very much and I think it would be unreasonable of me to expect you to start calling me by a name you reserve for her."

"Sometimes I miss my mom so much," Amy whispered. Tears formed in her wide blue eyes as she blindly grabbed a thick tome and dropped it into the box. "Why'd she have to go and die?"

"I wish I had an answer for that." Tannis knelt on the floor beside Amy and the half-full box. "Life is tough. I miss your mom, too. She was my very best friend, and I can't talk to anyone else like I could to her."

Amy hesitated. She wiped her eyes on her sleeve and gave Tannis a forlorn smile. "You could talk to me. Maybe sometimes we could talk about her, too."

"Thank you." Tannis hugged her. "Of course we can talk about your mother. I hope you and I will always be able to talk, Amy."

She thought for a brief moment that they'd weathered their first deep discussion, but then a troubled look crossed Amy's face again.

"Tannis, I like you, but I feel . . . funny about you marrying Dad. It's like he forgot all about Mom. If she was alive, you'd just be our neighbor."

Tannis nodded. "I think it's normal for you to feel odd about it. You feel like I'm replacing your mother."

Amy nodded. "Yeah. Sort of. Now that my dad loves you, will he forget Mom?"

That was a sticky one. How did she explain to a twelve-year-old that Tom didn't love her? That he was marrying her for steady sex and companionship? Tannis cleared her throat. "Your dad—and you, and Jeb and I—will never forget your mom, Amy. She lives in all of our memories and we'll have to share them with each other to keep her close to us. But your mom can't be here any more to help your dad be a good parent. That's something I can help him with. And your dad has needs, too—''

"You mean like sex." Amy nodded sagely.

Tannis almost strangled on her embarrassment. So this was what having an adolescent daughter was going to be like! "That's one thing, but I was thinking more of your dad's need for someone to support him, someone to share his life with.''

There was a thoughtful pause while Amy digested that. Tannis mentally girded herself for further explanations, but finally Amy smiled at her. "I never thought about it like that. I guess Dad does get pretty lonely. I feel that way sometimes, because I'm the only girl in our house. It'll be nice to have you live with us—you can be on my side when Dad and I get into arguments.''

Tannis give Amy a weak smile. Silence seemed to be the wisest answer to that statement. Tom came into the room then, and she almost leapt up and hugged him in sheer relief. What was she letting herself in for? She had no experience at mothering and her own relationship with her mother was nothing to fashion a role model from.

She went back to teaching the following Monday. She felt almost fully recovered, although she was exhausted by the end of the day, more from her colleagues twittering about her surprise engagement than from handling thirty active nine-year-olds.

On the Wednesday before the wedding, Tom drove her up to Culpeper to visit her mother. Tannis had called her over a week ago to tell her that she was getting married and had promised to visit before the wedding. Then, toward the end of the week, her mother's doctor had called and requested a meeting, so she'd set a time for Wednesday afternoon as soon as she could get there after school.

Driving into the parking lot of the nursing home, Tom looked around with appreciation. "Wow. If the inside is as gracious as this, I can see why it's important to you to keep her here."

"It's a lovely place." Tannis pointed to the left. "That whole area is a lovely little rock garden with walking paths and benches for the residents who are able to move around freely. Inside, there's an enclosed courtyard where they take patients who might wander."

Tom opened the front door of the facility and ushered her into the lobby.

Tannis saw it all again through his eyes, the hanging plants and tastefully arranged furnishings, and gratitude rose in her. "Thank you," she said, turning to clutch his sleeve. "It means so much to me to be able to keep her here."

Tom took her hand and linked her fingers through his. "You're right. It's really nice. And it doesn't smell like a hospital, either."

As they walked down the hallway toward her mother's room, Tannis savored the feel of her hand in Tom's. He'd touched her frequently in the past two weeks and she was growing accustomed to the low-level excitement he aroused in her with the most casual of caresses. He seemed to go out of his way to hold her hand or place his arm around her shoulders.

They'd had little private time together since they'd shared the news of their engagement with his children; most evenings he left her with a chaste peck on the lips, witnessed with avid interest by Amy and with youthful disgust by her little brother. Last night had been the only time Tom's control had slipped. He'd sent the children on ahead of him to get started with their baths. They were barely out the door when he'd pulled her into his arms and took her mouth with an absolute masculine demand she was helpless to resist.

Not that she'd wanted to.

More and more, she was beginning to realize that intimacy with Tom would be nothing like the lukewarm passion of her first marriage. His kisses started a fire inside her that his hands stoked effortlessly. Her body throbbed, her breath grew shallow, and in unguarded moments she caught herself standing motionless, staring blindly into space while she imagined the things Tom would do to her body. The thought of him filling her, moving in and against her, was enough to start a warm liquid feeling between her thighs and incite a restless urgency that pushed her into a frenzy of activity in order to forget it.

"Don't we need to talk to the doctor first?"

With a start, she realized they'd stopped outside the door of the doctor's office. She glanced up at Tom and found him looking down at her with an intense gaze that made her blush.

"Care to share that thought?" Although he wasn't smiling, there was a note of amusement in his tone.

She knew her face was pink, and having him read her so easily didn't help. "Not on your life," she muttered as she opened the door.

Her mother's doctor was easy to talk to. Although he was young enough to be her brother, he had a confident manner that reassured her that her mother was in good hands. And, most important, her mother liked him.

"Good afternoon, Mrs. Carlson." He shook her hand and looked at Tom expectantly.

"Dr. Payton, this is my fiancé, Tom Hayes," she said. It was the first time she'd had to introduce him that way, and the words sounded odd to her, almost as if she were telling an untruth.

Tom shook the doctor's hand. "You wanted to talk with us about Tannis's mother before we see her?"

"Yes." The doctor looked pensive. "Your mother's behavior has been somewhat...irrational this week. I want you to be prepared for sudden mood swings, unusual responses, even angry outbursts."

Tannis knew her face registered her dismay. "You mean more so than normal?"

The doctor gave her a sympathetic smile. "I'm afraid so." He turned to Tom. "Has Mrs. Carlson explained to you that her mother can be...difficult?"

Tom nodded when he appeared to expect a response, and the doctor turned back to Tannis.

"In our family counseling sessions over the past year, you've indicated that your mother appeared to be getting increasingly hostile. We've also begun to see this pattern emerge with the nurses and other staff members. After reviewing your mother's records, I'd like to recommend testing to find out if there's a physiological cause for her behavior."

"You think there's a reason she's getting meaner?" Her question was blunt, but the doctor only nodded. "What kind of tests are you considering? Would they be very intrusive?"

Dr. Payton shook his head. "Not intrusive in the sense that we'd be invading her body with surgery, but I'd like to do an MRI to see what we're dealing with. Of course, I'd need your signature."

Tannis mulled over his words. She looked at Tom, needing the strength she saw in his steady gaze. "What do you think?"

His answer was prompt. "If there's a chance that your mother is suffering from something treatable, I think you should take the opportunity to find out."

She nodded slowly. "You're right. Okay, Dr. Payton, I'll sign any permissions you need." She couldn't resist a wry smile. "But how you're going to explain all this to mother, I'll never know. She still thinks she's making all her own choices. What if she doesn't agree to the tests?"

Dr. Payton chuckled as he drew some papers from a folder in front of him. "I think I can present this to Madeline in a way that she'll accept. Let me give it a try before we start to worry about a 'what-if' that may never occur. I'll contact you after I speak to her, and if she agrees, we'll set up a date. If she refuses, we'll confer again before taking any action."

When the appointment ended, Tannis led Tom through the cheerful building to her mother's room. He'd deliberately taken her hand again the moment they left the doctor's office and he could feel the tension in her, wound as tight as a frantically ticking watch. As they drew closer to her mother's room, she gripped his hand tighter and tighter until her clasp was almost painful. He doubted she was even aware of it.

When they reached the hallway where her mother was, she carefully disengaged her hand. He didn't comment, but the small gesture spoke volumes. Just before they entered the room, she turned and stretched up to whisper in his ear.

"Be careful not to say anything about money to Mother. Although she did give me power of attorney on the recommendation of the doctor when she came here, she still believes that there's plenty of money from the house sale and her retirement."

"Okay." Tom put his hand over hers and squeezed. "I'll follow your lead." A feeling of remorse rose in him. How could he ever have doubted Tannis's commitment to her mother? She was going far out of her way to give her mother the impression that she was still in control of her life. He could imagine how important that illusion would be to someone elderly and ailing.

"Thanks." Tannis turned her hand over and squeezed his briefly in return. It was obvious she still dreaded exposing him to her mother. She squared her shoulders and knocked on the door. "I hope you're ready to enter the lion's den."

"It's not locked," called a distinctly querulous voice from inside the room.

Tannis pushed open the heavy door. As Tom followed, she approached a tiny dinette table at which a small, white-haired woman was sitting. The room was actually a small apartment and some of the tasteful antique furnishings had obviously come with the occupant. Once again, it hit him that his bride-to-be had made incredible sacrifices to ensure her mother's comfort.

"Hello, Mother." Tannis knelt and brushed a kiss across her parent's cheek before turning to draw Tom forward. "This is my fiancé, Tom Hayes. Tom, my mother, Madeline Ransom."

Tom stepped closer to the table as faded blue eyes that still resembled her daughter's scrutinized him from tip to toe. "It's nice to meet you, Mrs. Ransom. Tannis has spoken of you often."

The woman's eyes narrowed. "Nothing good, I'm sure."

"How have you been feeling this week, Mother?" Tannis rushed in before Tom could respond. "Is there anything I can bring you the next time I come up?"

Madeline Ransom's small hand shook as she pointed to a stack of books on a table next to the door. "I read all those. You could bring me some more. Guess you didn't think of that today. You don't ever think of me, do you? Now that I'm shut up in here, you just go on about your life and pretend I'm already dead and buried."

Tannis blanched and tears sprang to her eyes.

"Tannis has been very ill, Mrs. Ransom." Tannis shot him a pleading look, but Tom wasn't about to let her be slaughtered verbally like that. "She came very close to being hospitalized and she's only recently begun to teach again." He slid the bag he'd been carrying onto the table where the old lady could see it. "In here is some reading material Tannis brought for you, and we'll be happy to bring you some more on our next visit."

Madeline's face split in a delighted smile, all the venom and contrariness draining out of her in an instant. "Why, thank you, Mr. Hayes!" He'd swear she was flirting. "Maybe this marriage will be good for Tannis. You're as nice as Jeremy. She couldn't hold on to him, you know. Such a sloppy housekeeper. Why, you'd never know I taught that girl everything I knew about keeping a nice home for a man."

The comment should have irritated him, but the jarring switch to friendliness reminded him of what the doctor had said. Mrs. Ransom wasn't playing with a full deck. Realizing that made it easier for him to be courteous to her, and he jumped into the conversation several more times when the old lady turned on Tannis.

Finally, sensing Tannis was at the end of her rope by the strain in her voice, he drew her to her feet. "We have to be going now," he told her mother. "I don't know if Tannis told you, but I have two children. They'll be getting desperate for some supper before too long."

To his surprise, Mrs. Ransom offered him her hand. "I'll look forward to meeting them soon. After all, they may be the only grandchildren I ever have."

Don't count on it. The thought gave him a surprising amount of satisfaction as a picture of Tannis with his baby at her breast rose before him.

"Thank you for bringing Tannis," her mother went on. She shot a positively malevolent look at her daughter. "Perhaps you can persuade her to visit more regularly."

It was an unfair cut, considering he knew everything Tannis was doing to ensure her mother's comfort, but he forced himself to remember the doctor's words. "I'm sure I won't need to do any persuading. Tannis thinks of you every day."

Before Mrs. Ransom could spew any more poison in Tannis's direction, Tom ushered her out of her mother's apartment. In the hallway, Tannis leaned against the wall. She appeared almost oblivious to his presence, and he could see the immense battle going on inside her as she struggled not to break down.

Finally she took a deep breath and looked up at him. Her eyes were still shiny with unshed tears, but they also were wary and her expression was closed. "I'm sorry you had to play referee. She was in rare form today."

He wanted to take her into his arms, to rub her back and promise her she'd never have to come here by herself again, but he sensed she couldn't accept that. "I didn't mind. I'm glad you didn't have to do that alone."

It was as if she didn't hear him. "If you marry me, this is what you'll be taking on. Are you sure you're ready for that kind of responsibility?"

He didn't even hesitate. "I'm sure. Besides, I'm marrying you, not her." When he added, "Thank God," she finally unbent enough to smile a little.

"Today was the worst she's ever been. Usually her insults are veiled references to my shortcomings, but today she really took off the gloves."

"It's a good thing I know she's ill." He took her arm and steered her toward the front door. "I wanted to punch her when she made you cry."

That started a giggle out of her. "Believe me, I've wanted to punch her from time to time. But somehow, today was easier. Knowing that she isn't responsible for what she's saying, that it might be a medical condition, makes it easier. Does that make sense?"

They were in the parking lot and he paused to unlock her door with the automatic mechanism. "Yeah. But this visit cured me of considering having her live with us."

She nodded vigorously and rolled her eyes in agreement, moving to one side so he could open her door. But as she leaned toward him, he was suddenly overwhelmed by an awareness of her femininity, and he felt himself stirring to arousal. He placed his hands at her hips, pulling her against him, relishing the heat of her soft body and anticipating the sweeter heat that they generated together. Her face registered surprise, but as always, she relaxed and leaned into him, placing her palms on his shoulders.

Part of her appeal was her unconditional response, he decided as he dropped his head and sought her mouth. That very first time he'd ever kissed her, she'd appealed to his sense of decency, but all the while her body had cuddled against his in a clear sign that she enjoyed his touch. And his body had remembered it ever since.

He kissed her deeply, demanding a response which he got in full measure. Her generous curves were pressed against him and he unbuttoned her wool coat, slipping his hand inside her jacket and palming her breast through the silky blouse she wore. His other hand slid around to clasp her buttock and pull her hard against him, and he thrust his tongue even deeper into her mouth as she squirmed against him, making his suit pants fit even tighter than they already felt.

"Tom!" She jerked her mouth from his and pulled at his hand. "We're in a public parking lot! What are you doing?"

"Saturday can't get here soon enough for me," he said, and his voice was so deep and rough it didn't even sound like his. "I want you in my bed. I want to strip you naked and pull you down under me. I want to kiss you all over. I want to make you—"

Tannis stopped him by placing her palm over his mouth. He was gratified to note that her hand was shaking and her cheeks were fiery red. She dropped her head against his chest and he could see her vulnerable nape underneath the pinned coil in which she'd worn her hair today.

His body was rock-hard already, pushing him to disregard anything in search of satisfaction, but he resisted. Three more days and he could spend the whole night worshiping her pretty body, pouring himself into the warm chalice of her thighs—he was driving himself crazy! Three days seemed like an eternity. Sliding his hands from beneath her coat, he took her by the shoulders and pressed a kiss to the exposed spot at the back of her neck. "Let's go home."

Six

———

One day to go. Tomorrow, she'd be married. It hardly had seemed real until today. Tannis turned and walked back into the school with the other teachers as the last bus pulled away. In her classroom, there were signs of a party.

Much to her amazement, the room mother for her class had organized a small celebration in honor of her impending wedding, and the class had taken up a collection for a gift. Several of the moms who volunteered to help with the students through the year also came in, bearing cupcakes and big smiles.

Tenderly Tannis lifted the wedding album that had been her gift from her students. There were spaces for the names of the bride and groom, their family trees, for a description of the wedding and for the guest list and gifts received. She smoothed a hand across the embossed leather cover. Although this had been a hasty decision, she was beginning to feel hopeful about the future. Tom had gone out of his way to make their relationship appear normal, and she was starting to accept that it was. In addition, she was determined to be the best wife that ever was. Tom had offered her far more than marriage; he'd offered her financial stability and the chance to live her dream of a family of her own. She owed him, and any way she could repay him would never be enough.

As she tidied her desk and stuffed papers to be graded into her book bag, she felt the familiar trembling in the pit of her stomach...the trembling that had been there for several days, growing stronger and more insistent every time she thought of what would occur between Tom and her on Saturday evening.

"Mrs. Carlson?" The intercom blared and she reached behind her desk to answer Janine, the school secretary.

"Yes?"

"Could you come to the faculty room for a short meeting with a parent, please?"

Meeting with a parent? Tannis fretted as she quickly gathered up her grade book and headed for the staff room. Mentally she reviewed the children in her class and wondered which of them had been having problems serious enough to warrant a conference with the principal and herself. She couldn't think of a single child. True, Jolie Wilkins—

"Surprise!"

Tannis stopped with her hand on the knob of the faculty room door, shocked beyond speech. Her coworkers were all crowded into the small room and on the table used for lunch, there was a large sheet cake and a punch bowl. The two large packages wrapped in the unmistakable silvers, pinks and whites of wedding paper peeped from under a lacy parasol, and three silver helium balloons bounced at the ceiling with white paper wedding bells dangling below them.

Quick tears sprang to her eyes and she summoned a tremulous smile for her beaming friends. "You guys are a sneaky bunch," she proclaimed. "I can't believe you did all this without me suspecting a thing!"

Janine laughed. "I was sure you'd never swallow that line about a parent meeting."

"Hook, line and sinker." She shook her head again. "What a surprise. Thank you."

"Don't thank us yet. These could be gag gifts." One of the other fourth-grade teachers pushed a chair forward while others passed the gifts her way.

The first box was large and flat. And heavy. The card proclaimed it was from the entire faculty. She fiddled with the bow, prolonging the anticipation until her co-workers prodded her to quit fooling around. When the paper was pulled away and the box came open, it revealed a round silver serving tray with Tom's and her names and Saturday's date engraved in the center.

She was stunned. Again she felt the tears arise. "Thank you all. This is too much."

"These quickie weddings are hell. You should have seen me explaining to the jewelry store manager why I was buying it Monday afternoon and he had to have it engraved by Friday morning!" The reading teacher rolled her eyes and the others laughed, giving Tannis a chance to wipe her eyes.

"Okay, open the second one."

She picked it up and read the card aloud. "This one's really for Tom. From your crazed fourth-grade cohorts."

Really for Tom... Tannis could feel a blush starting. Narrow-eyed, she looked over at her three closest friends in the school, her fellow fourth-grade teachers. "Is this what I think it is?"

"Open it and see," was all they would say.

As she carefully unwrapped the second package, the ribbon snapped.

"Uh-oh! You know what that means," caroled Janine. "A baby for every broken ribbon."

"Open that box, Tannis," someone else called. "I have a feeling that what's in it will give you a head start on making babies."

Her face felt as if it was on fire, but her heart gave a leap of hope that the silly prediction would come true. When she opened the box, clouds of sheer tissue obstructed her view. With painstaking care, she folded back layer after layer of tissue until everyone in the room was groaning. But when the final piece of tissue was removed, a collective sigh went up from the women gathered around her as she held up the gift. The few men in the room let out catcalls and wolf whistles.

The girls had bought her a negligee in pale peach. Floor-length and floating, it was trimmed in lace and accompanied by a robe of fabric as sheer as the gown. Even wearing both items of clothing, Tannis figured it would reveal far more than it would conceal. The thought of wearing it in front of Tom made her mouth so dry she could barely swallow. Waves of embarrassment swamped her, but she gave her friends a game smile. "This is beautiful."

"Tom can thank us later."

Janine took pity on Tannis then. "Okay, everybody, I have punch over here and Wilma will cut the cake. Better get in line behind Tannis if you want some."

Staggering up the walk from Tom's driveway an hour later laden with her book satchel and gifts, Tannis heard the front door open. She remembered that Tom had taken the day off to handle last-minute details for the wedding.

"What's all this?" He relieved her of several boxes and her book bag.

"My class got us a gift, and after school the faculty threw a surprise shower for me. There's cake in that white box."

Tom raised his eyebrows. "Nice. Gonna show me what you got?"

Tannis felt her cheeks heat yet again. "Go ahead and open them."

He put away her coat and book bag and set the cake on the counter, then fell on the boxes. "I love presents." As luck had it, he found the album and the silver tray first. "Wow! They must really like you."

"What's not to like?" She tried for flippancy as he drew the third box toward him and removed the lid. The butterflies in her stomach became large birds, vainly flapping their wings against unseen glass walls.

Tom didn't answer as he pulled the peach confection from its nest of tissue. The filmy fabric looked ridiculous in his large hands. As she watched, drymouthed and mesmerized, he drew it over one arm so that she could see the rough, dark hairs liberally sprinkled over his forearm through the sheer material. He raised his gaze to hers, and she felt she knew how a drop of water hitting a heated skillet felt . . . sizzled into nothingness.

Tom rose. The lingerie and box fell off his lap to drop unheeded to the floor. One step brought him before her, one motion pulled her firmly into contact with his tall frame. "One more day," he whispered, his lips so close to hers that she could feel them brushing the sensitive flesh. "One more day and then you'll be mine."

Her eyelids fluttered closed as he fit his lips over hers and took her deep into a kiss. *One more day . . .* She shivered, thinking of the wedding night to come. She wanted him so badly, but at the same time, she was wary of the physical domination he exerted over her with so little apparent effort. Tom was always the one who ended their episodes of frantic petting. He was the one who retained the last shreds of control, pulling away after he'd reduced her to a mindless puddle of wanting . . . thought faded as the sweet magic of his tongue seduced and the warmth of his palm found her breast.

Minutes later, the front door slammed. Jeb's youthful voice called, "Hi, Dad, I'm home!"

Tom lifted his head; she hung limp in his arms in total surrender. Without the addicting drug of his kiss, an echo of her thoughts returned to plague her. If he'd taken her here on the floor, now, she wouldn't have had the sense to protest.

But he'd cloaked himself again in that formidable control. Even as she acknowledged the unwelcome thought, he buttoned her blouse and released her just before Jeb came charging into the living room to show them his new baseball cards.

When she awoke on Saturday morning, she could hear rain beating a light, uneven tattoo against her window. Her gaze moved around the bedroom, the bare walls instantly reminding her that this was her wedding day. This would be the last morning she would wake up as a single person, the last morning of her life that she wouldn't have someone depending on her, someone needing her for some reason.

When she'd married Jeremy, she'd been full of dreams of family and forever. It had taken less than two years for him to destroy her faith in herself and the love she thought she'd felt for him. With Tom, there would be no such unpleasantness. No surprises.

Again, she looked around the sparsely furnished room. There wasn't much left in her house. In one week, Tom and the kids had helped her dispose of almost every single item she'd accumulated in over three decades of living. Oh, they'd moved box after box of personal possessions to her new home, but she'd kept very little of her furniture. Other than the antique desk that had been in her father's family, her grandmother's cedar chest and an old grandfather clock that her mother had gotten from her mother when she married, the only other furniture that they had decided to keep was her dining room set. Tom insisted it was in better shape than his after surviving two small children, but she suspected he'd simply wanted her to feel more comfortable about the move.

Sudden doubt assailed her. Was she crazy to think she could make this work? The stack of negatives loomed far higher than even the heated perfection of Tom's kisses in the cold light of her wedding morning. As she pulled the ivory silk suit she planned to wear from her closet, her stomach clenched in knots that owed more to distress than desire.

What if Tom was making a mistake in thinking she could fit into his family?

At ten minutes before eleven, Tom knocked on her door. She'd been ready and waiting, but her heart skipped up into her throat and made it difficult to breathe.

Slowly she twisted the knob and opened the door. His physical presence hit her with the force of a ten-foot wave and her insides felt as tumbled and tossed as a sea creature caught in the fierce tug-of-war of the tide.

He wore suits to work every day. She'd often seen him in a suit before, she told herself sternly.

But he'll be marrying you in this suit. The thought brought her heart down into place again, where it beat such a rapid rhythm she was afraid he could hear it.

He looked showered and freshly shaved. His dark hair gleamed with deep brown highlights and the suit in question embraced his broad shoulders perfectly. A pink rosebud was pinned to his lapel. It matched the bouquet he held in his hand and as he offered it to her, his green gaze wandered over her from the baby's breath she'd slipped into the simple French braid to the sleek, expensive ivory pumps she only wore on very dressy occasions.

Flustered by the possession she detected in that gaze, she reached out for the flowers.

"Thank you. These are perfect." And they were. Tom had brought her simple pink rosebuds stripped of their thorns and surrounded by elegant fronds of fern and baby's breath. A cascade of pink-and-ivory ribbon spilled from them. She held the bouquet to her nose to inhale the delicate perfume.

Tom cleared his throat. "Are you ready to get married?"

If she didn't know better, she'd think he was as nervous as she. But that was silly. What would he have to be nervous about, after all? She was the one who was swallowing her pride and allowing Tom to shoulder her responsibilities. She was the one who was taking on a ready-made family who might resent her trying to replace the woman who'd held the position originally. She was the one who was marrying a man who might never be able to love her the way she—

The way she what? Her hands clenched on the delicate blooms as the rest of her thought overrode the check she'd automatically placed on it.

The way she loved him.

Oh, God. She didn't dare look at Tom. How long? How long had she loved him? And how long had she denied it out of loyalty, first to Mary and later to her memory?

"Tannis? Are you ready?"

He didn't know what she was thinking, but the look on her face made him nervous as hell. Was she going to back out on him at this late hour?

Maybe it would be for the best. When he'd awoken this morning, the folly of what he was doing nearly smothered him. She could never replace Mary. He'd loved his wife so much. Remarriage seemed a betrayal of that love.

Particularly with Tannis. It wasn't just any woman he wanted to marry—it was this particular woman. He wanted Tannis worse than he could ever remember wanting a woman before, but that didn't mean he had to marry her. In fact, it was incredibly selfish of him to be so ecstatic about the thought of having her in his bed every night. And he did mean *having*. How could he do this to the kids? They'd never adjust to a stepmother. He'd never adjust to a wife. Other than Mary.

As he considered beating Tannis to the punch, asking her if she thought they were being a bit hasty in considering marriage, she bit her lip and aimed a tremulous smile in the direction of his Adam's apple.

"I'm ready." Her voice was soft, as soft as the sweet curves of her body, and he was ashamed of how easily his hormones trampled his common sense.

His hormones replied. "Good. Amy and Jeb are waiting in the car."

His hormones escorted her out under an umbrella and opened the door, watching hungrily as her dress caught on the fabric of the seat and pulled taut across her thighs for a moment.

And his hormones led him around to the driver's side, where he slid in and started the brief journey to the chapel, where he was going to marry this woman simply because he wanted her too badly to do anything else. And because the mere thought that another man might see the fire hidden deep inside her if he didn't get her under lock and key made him gnash his teeth.

The pastor and his wife met them at the chapel and without any great ceremony, they all filed inside. It wasn't until the man began to intone the familiar words that Tom realized just how difficult this part was going to be.

In his heart, Mary was standing at his side. In his heart, he was a young man in love for the first time, with a future filled with happiness ahead. In the future he'd envisioned on his first wedding day, there had been no room for ugly words like, "cancer," and "terminal," and "widower."

When it came time for him to affirm his pledge to the woman he was taking in marriage, he couldn't look at Tannis. The grief he thought he'd conquered had him in an iron grip. He stared straight ahead as he gritted out, "As long as we both shall live," and listened in stony silence as the minister repeated the vows for his bride.

He slipped the ring Jeb handed him onto her finger at the appropriate time and waited while Amy handed her the one he'd chosen. Silently he noted that her hands were icy though he never looked at her once.

When the ceremony was over—thank God it had been brief—they signed the marriage certificate, accepted the congratulations of the reverend and his wife and then went back out into the pouring rain and drove to the restaurant where he'd made reservations for a celebratory lunch. It was an effort to act normal, but he must have been reasonably successful because Amy and Jeb didn't appear to notice anything wrong. In fact, they were both in such high spirits that he and Tannis were barely required to contribute anything to the conversation, which suited him fine.

Memories of his life with Mary were bombarding him, pelting his consciousness with the relentless steady rhythm of the raindrops falling outside. He *had* loved her.

His one unforgivable lapse came back to haunt him now and he found himself almost resenting the woman across the table from him. He knew he and Mary had had one of their first serious arguments about the course of treatment she should seek for her recently diagnosed illness. But he couldn't remember their words.

On the other hand, he remembered every small detail of walking Tannis home...his awareness of her lush curves silhouetted in the moonlight...the forced intimacy he'd felt on her small covered porch. She'd seemed so warm and giving, and he'd been so terrified that Mary was going to leave him. He'd hated himself immediately afterward, but for the few minutes she'd allowed him to kiss her, he'd been completely sure that she was as involved as he was.

But it still galled him that she had been the one to call a halt. He could still hear her words as she'd pressed firmly against his shoulders.

"Tom, I find you very attractive. But we both care about Mary. This would hurt her terribly."

And she'd been right. It had been wrong then, and it still felt wrong today.

After the luncheon, they went back to the house. Amy and Jeb helped Tannis retrieve the few things she still needed from her old house and install her in the master bedroom, then in midafternoon he drove them to the homes of the friends with whom they planned to spend the night.

It had been his idea to spend their first night together alone without the kids, to have some privacy, but as he stepped through the front door, he loathed the silence.

Tannis came out of the kitchen. She had a spoon in her hand. "I thought I'd make some soup and let it simmer this evening. That way we'll have a meal for one night this week. I know mealtime will be hectic with all the different activities we have scheduled."

"You don't have to cook," he said, more gruffly than he'd intended. "I didn't marry you for your housekeeping skills."

Did she flinch or was it his imagination?

She looked away. "I like to cook."

He thrust a hand through his hair. What now? He'd planned to take her out for a nice meal somewhere, then bring her home and take her to bed.

But the idea of seducing Tannis held no appeal tonight.

Suddenly he needed to be alone. He couldn't stand here and make small talk with *his wife* another minute. "I brought home some work. I'll be in the office if you need me." He turned away before she could answer and stomped into his office, slamming the door.

He stayed there for the rest of the afternoon and eventually he was able to immerse himself in his work. He heard her moving around a few times and just before six o'clock she went upstairs. He never heard her come down again.

At nine-thirty, he finally gave up his struggle to maintain any pretense of interest in the work before him. What the hell was she doing up there? For the past hour, he'd heard her walking around, opening and closing doors...surely she wasn't *housecleaning?*

Out of nowhere came a vivid image of her face as he looked down at her just before he took her mouth. Soft, giving...she hadn't been trying to salve his ego all those years ago when she said she'd found him attractive. No woman could be that good an actress.

Guilt followed hard on the heels of the sensual reverie. He'd been a real cad today. Yes, he'd been missing Mary but perhaps Tannis had her own ghosts to conquer. This was the time to let go of the past and look to their life together. Hibernating in his office, neglecting his bride on her wedding day wasn't the way to start out. He swallowed. An apology was in order.

Slamming his pen down on the legal pad before him with more force than necessary, he yanked open the door of the office and took the stairs two at a time. Just as he cleared the landing and turned the corner at the top, the door of the guest bathroom opened and Tannis stepped out.

She was wearing a thick, fluffy robe of some flowered material and her face was scrubbed clean of makeup though her hair was still braided and dressed as it had been for the wedding ceremony.

While the robe was certainly pretty enough, it wasn't the sheer peach confection he'd been imagining. But what really stopped him in his tracks was the small cool smile she gave him as she swept past him and entered the guest bedroom. "Good night."

"Good night? What the hell—Tannis, this is our *wedding* night!"

The door closed. And he heard the click of the lock from the inside. Her voice sounded flat and cold. "I'm surprised you remember."

It dawned on him that the noises he'd heard had been her moving her things into the guest bedroom. Inexplicably he was furious. Never mind the fact that he'd been the one keeping his distance from her all day: she was his wife now. And she was going to sleep with him. *Stop it. Hayes. Who do you think you'll impress with a caveman routine?*

It took a mighty effort, but he clamped a tight lid on the rage. Tannis didn't deserve it. The things that had him so worked up inside weren't her fault, and it wasn't fair to use her as a convenient scapegoat.

He raised a hand and forced himself to knock gently on the door she'd just shut in his face. "Tannis? Would you please come out for a minute?"

For a moment there was no answer and he thought she might ignore him, then she opened the door again.

She had just started to take the baby's breath out of her hair. Her eyes were wide and shadowed and in them he clearly read hurt.

"I'm sorry." He blew out a sigh of equal parts frustration and self-loathing. "Today was . . . tougher than I'd expected. Would you like to take a dip in the hot tub with me?" It was all he could manage. He couldn't promise to talk, to communicate or to tell her anything more, but she must have seen how much it took for him to get out even that much, because after a pause that seemed to last hours, she nodded.

"Let me change into a suit and I'll be down."

* * *

Tom was already in the bubbling water when she entered the basement where his hot tub was located. *Their* hot tub, she corrected herself. This was their home now.

Deliberately not allowing herself to focus on the hurt that brewed deep inside, she said, "This will be wonderful—having a hot tub inside. It's the thing I liked least about mine, having to go out in subzero weather to use it in the winter."

She hated having him watch her as she climbed into the tub with all the grace she could manage. She might have lost some weight but she was no more confident about her body than she'd ever been. Compared to Mary, she was...well padded was a kind way to phrase it.

As she sank into the water across from Tom, she surprised a grin on his face. It was so unexpected after his blue moodiness earlier, that she demanded, "What's so funny?"

"Nothing." His voice was nonchalant. "I was just wondering why you wore a suit tonight when you usually don't bother."

"Why I wore..." Her eyes widened and her mouth dropped open. "Have you been *spying* on me? That's the lowest, sneakiest thing I've ever heard—"

"Whoa." Tom was laughing so hard he could barely speak as he put his hands on her shoulders and pulled her through the water onto his lap. "I couldn't figure out how to tell you. I knew you were going to be mad—"

"*Mad?* 'Mad' doesn't begin to describe the way I feel about being ogled when I thought I was alone."

She could count on one hand the number of times she'd ever seen his hard face creased in uninhibited laughter. The expression altered his usual forbidding look—he looked more approachable, almost handsome. His legs were warm and rough with hair beneath her thighs but she sat stiffly, refusing to be seduced by the sheer masculine appeal he exuded. The hurt that had grown inside her throughout the long afternoon when it appeared her new husband had forgotten her very existence helped to fuel her righteous indignation now. "I can't believe you did that. I'm self-conscious about my body already and now I find out you've been critiquing it while I—"

"Tannis. I liked what I saw. I liked it a lot." The dancing light in his eyes dimmed and his expression sobered. "I knew it was wrong, but I...I couldn't help myself."

His honesty disarmed her. And when she allowed the anger to slip for a minute, she immediately was conscious of a warm, breathless amazement. Tom sounded as if he really liked her body. When he drew her closer, she didn't resist.

"I've always been incredibly attracted to you. I dreamed about these—" He placed a big, warm palm directly over one breast. "About touching you here, seeing these pretty nipples pouting for me." He looked into her eyes again. "I know you're physically attracted to me, too. The way I feel can't be all one-sided. Come here and let me show you how good we can be together."

Some kernel of independence inside her resisted him, unwilling to forgive him completely for what had occurred earlier, but it was as if he read her mind.

"I'm sorry if you felt ignored. I had to work some things out in my mind before I could...be with you."

It wasn't much, but loving him as she did, it was all she needed. When he put a dripping finger beneath her chin, she allowed him to tilt her face up and fit his mouth over hers in a sweet, sure blending that she felt she'd been without for a hundred years. The feelings roiling inside her burst into an inferno of flame. This was Tom, the man she loved. She was finally here, right where she wanted to be, and she was foolish to allow her pride to stand in the way of their life together.

He was leisurely at first, tracing the outline of her lips with a delicate touch of his tongue, gradually deepening the caress until he was bathing every inner surface with swift, penetrating strokes that lit fires deep within her. She was sitting upright on his lap, and he settled his hands at the curve of her waist. As the stiffness left her body, he slipped his hands around her back and applied subtle, steady pressure until the distance between them was gone and she was leaning against him, her breasts crushed against the hard, muscled planes of his chest.

Her suit was wet. It felt as if there was hardly anything separating her bare, wet skin from his, but still, when he put a hand to the shoulder strap of her one-piece suit and dragged down the stretchy fabric until a breast popped free, she tore her mouth from his and hid her face in his shoulder.

He freed her other breast and she could barely breathe for the huge bubble of sheer sexual excitement lodged in her chest. Tom took her by the shoulders, pulling her away from his body and she was stunned by the hot, wild desire in his hungry gaze as she rolled the suit the rest of the way over her hips, down her legs and tossed the sodden piece of cloth onto the concrete floor.

It was obvious—more than obvious that he wanted her. And in a small part of her heart there flowered a dream...if he desired her, if he was so enthralled with her body, maybe someday he'd come to love her, too.

"I've dreamed of this for so long." His voice was a gutteral whisper as he cupped one warm mound in his hand and slowly, steadily rubbed a thumb back and forth across her nipple. He watched intently as it peaked beneath his hand, then he picked up the tempo until he was flicking his thumb across her and she was beginning to breathe in short pants. Just as she thought she couldn't bear any more, Tom bent his head and she braced herself for an onslaught of sensation.

When his mouth closed over the taut crest he'd created, she gasped and arched against him. A hot sliver of need bloomed just above the apex of her legs and between them an insistent ache tormented her, growing larger and more demanding with each lap of the heated water over her sensitized skin.

As if he knew what torment she was enduring, Tom swept a hand down her body, faithfully following the contours of waist and hip and outer thigh. Then his fingers made a stealthy foray around to the inside of her upper leg, where he paused, tracing tiny patterns until she couldn't take it any longer. With a whispered, "Please," she moved her legs apart, inviting a more intimate touch.

Tom didn't disappoint her. Slowly, deliberately, he smoothed a hand up the inside of her thigh. She felt as if she were an elastic band being stretched tighter and tighter and tighter... and when he finally found the soft, secret flesh that throbbed and ached for his touch, she cried out and pushed herself against his hand. He sought, circled, stroked until she was mindlessly lifting her hips against his fingers repeatedly.

When he took his hand away, she whimpered and went limp in his arms. "What... why..." But before she could voice the question, the water in the tub boiled into a maelstrom of movement and she realized he'd turned on the jets.

His hand returned almost at once and she was immediately caught up in the rhythmic sensations of the sensual quest again. Beneath her buttock, she could feel his hard arousal and dimly she wondered why he was waiting. All thought ceased a moment later when he probed her sensitive passage with a long finger.

She spread her legs and lifted herself toward that seeking finger and Tom took full advantage of her wordless offer. As he did so, he lifted her body slightly, angling her toward the wall of the tub and she was stunned by a rush of water bubbling over the swollen, sensitive nub he'd called forth. The water's caress was too, too much and she felt a powerful wave cresting inside her, lifting and tossing her atop its foaming edge until she gave in to the pulsing rush and run of the water and the hot glide of his finger within her depths. She convulsed in his arms, only dimly aware of Tom muttering. "That's it, baby, let go. Let go," in her ear.

She was drained when the powerful climax finally subsided, totally limp in his arms. But Tom didn't give her any time to recover. He stood in the tub, keeping a strong arm around her back so that her legs slithered down to twine with his in the water. His mouth sought hers again and he kissed her so hard that he bent her backward over his arm. Then he pulled slightly away from her. She felt his other hand between them and she realized that he was pulling down his own swim trunks. Her body registered the hard length of his aroused flesh as it pressed against her belly. She glanced down, startled, and was immediately mesmerized by the sight of his full arousal sandwiched between his coarse dark hair and her own nest of soft, curly red.

Tom didn't give her time to appreciate the sight. She felt his hands at her waist and he lifted her. As she did so, he pushed his hips forward, sliding her down against him and impaling her on his strong shaft. Without a second's hesitation she locked her legs around his hips and placed her hands on his shoulders, allowing him to govern her movements and his own.

Tom groaned.

She relaxed, sinking more fully onto him and he groaned again. The sound echoed in the small room; when it died away it seemed to take with it the last shreds of his self-control. With a low animal sound of need, he threw back his head. At the same time, he began a rapid thrust and tug within her, holding her hips in place with his big hands.

She found herself totally enveloped, overwhelmed by his timing, his big body, his hard hands and his hot chest. Each time he slammed himself against her, another small flame burst into life within her, adding to her rising excitement as she watched his face. Beneath her, the lick of the bubbling water caressed her naked buttocks. She hadn't thought it possible, but as she rode him to his racking completion in her arms, she found a second shattering release that rendered her oblivious to anything but the warm water closing around them as Tom's legs gave way and he sank back onto a seat in the hot tub.

They rested there for a moment, her head against his chest, bodies still intimately entwined. But the water now was as uncomfortably sweltering as it had been soothing minutes before.

"Let's go to bed." Tom lifted her off his lap, sighing as he slid free of her. "You feel so good. If this water wasn't so hot, I could have stayed there all night."

"Mmm, hmm." She smiled as he assisted her out of the tub and wrapped her possessively in her terry-cloth robe, too drained to do more than agree. Her smile grew wider as she recalled how she worried about pleasing him, about her own responses to his handling.

Tom looked relaxed, more so than she'd ever seen him and the memory of his loss of control warmed her inside. He'd been nearly wild for her... after he'd finally come out of the lair she envisioned inside his office.

Now she realized anew how difficult this day must have been for him. He'd goaded her into anger when she'd first joined him, she remembered, and then he'd teased her out of it. Perhaps that had been what he needed to take his mind off comparisons between this wedding night and his first. If their lovemaking had been as shattering for him as it had for her, he hadn't been comparing anything. She was glad she'd been able to bring him physical satiation, at least.

He wrapped a towel haphazardly around his hips and put an arm around her, guiding her up to the bedroom and the wide mahogany bed she would share with him now.

Seven

In the silence of the night, she woke to find his hand already between her legs, his mouth a sensual torment at her breast. Drowsy, swamped in sensation, she rolled onto her back and slipped her hand between their bodies, searching out his hardening masculinity, reveling in the silky, smooth feel of his pulsing, leaping flesh. He allowed her caresses for a few minutes, then took her hands in one big fist and stretched them above her head. Nudging her knees apart, he knelt between her thighs and entered her in one long, smooth stroke.

It was perfect. The room was dark and cool around them but beneath the blankets they were wrapped in a cocoon of heat. His back was slick with sweat beneath her palms, his body demanding a response she gave helplessly. When his rhythm increased and he began to groan with each rushing breath, he slipped his hand between their bodies and lightly, repeatedly rolled her sensitive woman flesh beneath his finger until she convulsed around him, her soft channel squeezing his length as he followed her into spasms of fulfillment.

He dropped back off to sleep moments later, after wrapping his arms around her and rolling them over so that she was pillowed on his body and he was still a part of her.

"I told you I could stay here all night," he said, sleepily claiming her mouth for a final kiss.

She was happier than she'd ever been in her life, sprawled over his hard body with her head cradled on his shoulder. This was how she'd always sensed it could be with Tom—this white-hot-sexuality that burned through every restraint she'd tied around her heart. But it was frightening, too.

Much as she wanted to kid herself, she hadn't married Tom for money or for babies, or even for the sex, great as it had turned out to be. She married Tom because she loved him...had loved him silently for years, though she hadn't admitted it even to herself.

And it was terrifying because she knew he didn't love her.

He recognized the mouth-watering smell of lasagna as soon as he walked in the door. As Tom set his briefcase inside his office, Tannis came around the corner from the kitchen. She'd begun to greet him at the door every evening. His contentment deepened.

"Hi. Dinner will be ready in about five minutes." She gave him a quick kiss, then smiled when he caught her around the waist and pulled her back for a deeper exploration of her mouth.

They'd been married only two weeks and he hadn't gotten nearly enough of her yet.

"I told you that you don't have to cook every night."

"And I told you I wouldn't. But Jeb's ball game starts at six and I thought we wouldn't be so rushed if I got something ready."

"Thanks." He lowered his head to kiss her again, relishing the feel of her pliant body against him. He'd missed a woman's softness more than he'd realized. Marrying her had been one of his better ideas, and he was determined to show her how much her presence in his life meant to him.

"Tannis? Is my uniform clean?" Jeb clattered down the steps from the second floor and Tom sighed and released her.

She looked as if she regretted the interruption as much as he did, but she turned with a smile for his son. "It's in the dryer now. Why don't you go see if it's dry?"

As Jeb skidded around the corner and bounded down the basement steps, Amy came out of the dining room. "Tannis, I finished my English homework. Daddy, why do I have to go along to Jeb's stupid ball game tonight?"

"Hi, Ame. It's nice to see you, too." Tom's voice was wry. He felt like he barely made it in the door at night before his daughter was provoking some new conflict.

Amy dropped her belligerent stance enough to smile at his unspoken rebuke. "Hi, Daddy." Then she crossed her arms and the smile faded. "So why do I have to go? Half the time Jeb can't even catch the ball."

"That's unfair, Amy." Tom sighed and set his briefcase inside the door of his office. "Jeb is almost six years younger than you are and he does his best."

"Big deal." The twelve-year-old tossed her high ponytail. "I still hate those games. Why can't I stay home?"

"We've discussed this before. I don't feel comfortable leaving you alone at home for several hours in the evening."

Amy's face flushed red with anger. "You treat me like a baby! Tannis wouldn't make me go, I bet." She turned her gaze toward her stepmother, clearly pleading for feminine intervention.

Tannis hesitated. "You feel you're too old to have to go along to Jeb's ball games every week?"

Amy nodded vigorously. "They're stupid."

"You want to stay home?"

Another nod. Clearly sensing a potential victory, the girl added, "I'd be good, I promise."

Tom snorted. He wasn't at all pleased with the way Tannis appeared to be on the verge of giving in. Amy was *not* staying home tonight.

"We trust you," Tannis said. "I'm sure you would use good judgment." Then she glanced at Tom, gauging his expression.

He stared back at her without moving a muscle. Irritation began to gel into anger. She should know better than to countermand his decisions in front of Amy.

Tannis turned back to Amy. "I suggest a compromise. Amy, you want to be allowed to try something new. Your dad has concerns about what you want to do."

She glanced at him again and he could see she was pleading for his understanding. "We don't have time tonight to discuss this whole issue. Could we set a time, maybe tomorrow night when there's no game, to sit down and talk about this? Maybe then we could come to some kind of agreement that you both could live with."

He didn't like it at all. But he had to admit his dealings with Amy lately hadn't produced many positive results. Maybe he should try it Tannis's way. "I'm willing to talk about this some more tomorrow night. But don't get your hopes up," he warned Amy.

"I guess we can talk about it," she conceded. Then, as if none of what Tannis had said had penetrated her consciousness, Amy said, "So what about tonight? Can I stay home?"

"Not tonight." Tannis jumped into the pause before he gave in to the urge to roar. "Why don't you bring a book along to pass the time?"

Amy's brows drew together in a dark line that he recognized from his own expression when he shaved every morning. "I don't want to read a book! I'm old enough to stay by myself and I don't want to go to any stupid little-kid ball game!" She stomped off with deliberate, earthshaking steps.

In the silence that followed, Tannis shook her head and gave him a small, worried smile. "So much for my attempt to defuse the situation."

"But you have a point." It was hard for him to realize that he didn't have to do all the child-rearing on his own now, and tonight was a prime example. "I guess I need to be more flexible. I don't like the thought of Amy staying home by herself, but perhaps we should talk about it sometime."

"Tomorrow night. With her."

"Yeah." He exhaled, not looking forward to what he suspected would turn into yet another shouting match. "I'll set the table if you'll help Jeb find his uniform."

After dinner, they all went to the ballpark. Amy brought along a popular teen romance in which she buried her head as soon as he set up lawn chairs for Tannis and Amy beside the hard wooden benches designed for spectators. Tannis had a bagful of school papers that she immediately pulled out and began to grade, but he knew from seeing her here last week that the moment Jeb took the field she would lay down her work and cheer him on. A warm, contented feeling swelled inside him as he followed Jeb down to the dugout. Tannis had fit into his bed as if she'd been made for him. Now she was fitting into his family even better than he'd expected, as well.

He picked up a bat and stuck several balls in his jacket pockets. As one of the team's assistant coaches, he'd been surprised to discover how much he enjoyed helping these little fellows work on their throwing, catching and hitting. The only fly in the ointment had been his concern about what Amy might get into while his attention was on the game, and with Tannis to keep an eye on her, that was no longer a worry.

"Hayes! If I had a new wife, I can think of better places to be than the ball field." It was one of the other coaches.

Tom grinned. "So can I, Chub, but our family commitments took precedence."

Chub shook his head in dismay and pushed his cap back on his balding head. "You didn't even take her on a honeymoon. What's the world coming to? I'm disappointed in you, Hayes. Don't you know women need romance?"

"I'm romantic." Tom defended himself. "Just because I didn't take her on a honeymoon doesn't mean I flunked Romance 101."

"Did you send her flowers on your one-week anniversary? Have you taken her out for a special dinner with no kids where you two exchange meaningful looks and drool all over the tablecloth? Have you bought her a new negligee to replace the one you ripped off her in a fit of passion on your wedding night?"

Tom was laughing as he took a small group of six-year-olds into the outfield to chase flies, but his amusement faded quickly. Maybe there was some truth to Chub's words. He hadn't done anything extra special for his wife. It had simply never occurred to him to bring her flowers, and since the fiasco of his wedding night, he hadn't even *seen* the peach negligee she'd received from her co-workers. Tom didn't consider himself a coward, but there were some topics an intelligent man knew better than to bring up with his wife.

His mouth hardened into a firm line as he popped the first ball up and watched a little kid scramble for it. Chub was right. Tannis deserved a little romance in this relationship. He'd remedy that tomorrow.

* * *

"How do you pronounce *b-o-u-d-o-i-r?*"

Tannis took her gaze from the field long enough to smile quizzically at Amy. "*'Boo-dwahr.'* Is that in your book?"

"Yep." Amy went back to reading.

Tannis stared at her a moment longer, wondering exactly what Amy was reading. Then she shrugged and grinned. She'd have to share that exchange with Tom later. Who knew what went on in the mind of an adolescent girl?

She turned her attention back to the game. Jeb hadn't started, but after three innings the coach put him into right field. Now it was the top of the fifth inning and Jeb's team was at bat. The first batter slapped a weak hit right into the second baseman's glove. As he ran for first base, the second baseman threw wild and the first baseman ran to pick it up while the runner scampered on to second. The second batter, a big, husky seven-year-old, drilled a line drive out toward third. It got by the third baseman and zipped into left field and the runner got to second before the left fielder could get the ball to the infield to cover him. Now it was Jeb's turn to bat.

He swung and missed the teed-up ball the first time. She called encouragement from her seat and even Amy put down her book to yell for him. The second time Jeb swung at the ball with all the energy in his young body. It didn't connect squarely, but he managed to dribble a grounder into the infield. Tannis jumped to her feet and screamed along with the other parents who were cheering for Jeb. He ran as fast as his little legs would carry him toward first base, but the shortstop scooped up the ball and threw it to the first baseman, who caught it moments before Jeb crossed the base.

As he trudged back across the field to his dugout, Tannis could see disappointment in every line of his dejected figure. Still, she was proud that he'd hit the ball and she could see from the gentle pat Tom gave him on the back that he was equally tickled.

The inning ended and Jeb's team prepared to take the field. He looked so little standing way out there in the grass with his mitt dangling from his hand and his uniform bagging around his scrawny figure that she felt tears spring to her eyes. It seemed like only yesterday he'd been a screaming red-faced baby. If only Mary could see him now.

Mary. She'd avoided thinking of Mary for the past few weeks. Not because she felt guilty—in fact, the opposite was true. She truly believed that Mary would be happy about this marriage. Not just for the sake of the children, but for Tom and her, as well. She'd needed him. So much more than she'd ever understood, she needed him.

And that was why she hadn't wanted to think of Mary. Tom didn't need her, Tannis. Oh, he might enjoy the willing warmth of her body, and he might appreciate her help and input in the daily routine of his household, but emotionally, he didn't need her. She'd hoped that he might begin to share something of himself—of his hopes, his feelings, his dreams. But she very much feared that he was still sharing those things with Mary in the silence of the night when he lay beside her, and she knew from the restless movements of his big body that he wasn't sleeping.

Perhaps she was expecting too much too soon.

Her attention was drawn back to the field as the teams switched places. The first batter up for the opposing team was an experienced eight-year-old who was their star hitter. He cracked a high fly straight out toward right field on the very first swing. Tannis stood and shaded her eyes from the late-evening sun as she watched Jeb run forward and back, weaving uncertainly as he tried to get under the ball. As the ball descended, he lunged forward with his mitt outstretched.

The ball hit him squarely in the forehead.

She was already on her feet, dashing behind the fence out toward the outfield by the time his little body hit the ground. He lay still, very still. Her heart was in her throat and she was vaguely aware of Amy pounding along behind her.

Tom beat her to him. He dropped to his knees and spoke to his son. "Jebbie? Jeb, talk to me."

She could hear the raw fear in his voice and her heart shrank in pain and panic. Then Jeb's foot moved.

The world began to move at normal speed again, and she sagged in relief. As she got closer, he groaned and tried to sit up with groggy, half-formed motions. Tom pressed him back. One of the mothers was a general surgeon. She examined Jeb while another of the coaches came puffing up with an ice pack.

Tannis could see that Jeb's forehead was already swelling into an enormous purpling knot, but he was talking and moving his hands around. The tension inside her eased as the doctor said, "No sign of concussion, little buddy. In a couple of days you should be as good as new."

Beside her, Amy's voice quavered. "Is Jebbie okay?"

Tannis put an arm around the girl's shoulders, understanding the fear. The child had lost a member of her family already—a frightening event like this could destroy her sense of security. "I think he'll be fine, honey. He's going to have a heck of a goose egg, though."

Lifting Jeb into his arms, Tom glanced up and caught her eye. "Can you get our things together? I'll bring Jeb and meet you at the car."

She nodded. "Rest would probably be the best thing for him right now."

Amy snorted, her preadolescent bravado restored with the reassurance that her brother was going to live to plague her another day. "Betcha we go to the hospital before we go home. Dad thinks every little bruise is a major wound."

Tannis smiled at her. "But he's already gotten the A-OK from a doctor."

"Won't matter."

She was right. Tom called Dr. Ellis, who met them at the Emergency Room. After thoroughly looking Jeb over, he convinced Tom that other than a slight headache, Jeb would be fine. He reminded them of signs of head injury to watch for, refilled Jeb's ice pack and released him.

By the time they got home, it was the children's bedtime.

When Tom came downstairs after checking on his son one last time, she was just finished grading the spelling tests that she'd dropped when the ball hit Jeb.

He flopped down beside her on the sofa. "He looks okay for now. I'll set my alarm clock and check on him every hour or so tonight and we'll see if he's well enough to go to school tomorrow."

Tannis smiled fondly at his concern. "I doubt you need to look in on him that frequently. Little boys recuperate quickly. I'm sure he'll be raring to go to school in the morning to show all his friends his bruise."

"We'll see how he is in the morning," Tom said with a note of finality in his tone.

"You've been a single parent for too long." She deliberately infused her voice with a note of light humor, inviting him to laugh with her. "You should hear how overprotective you sound."

"I don't give a damn how overprotective I sound! No one in my family is ever going to die of neglect again." His voice was harsh and loud in the quiet family room.

Her hands stilled on the papers she held. He was far more upset than this accident should have warranted...and angry, too. Had she said something that he'd misconstrued?

"Die of neglect—are you talking about Mary?" She tried to make sense of his heated words. "You were with Mary constantly. Tom, she didn't die because you neglected her."

"I didn't challenge the decision she made to forgo treatment, did I? I didn't insist that she go for chemotherapy...."

She was dumbfounded. A bitter anger burned through his words. She'd had no idea he blamed himself for Mary's death. Was that why he lay awake at night?

Gently, reaching for words, she shook her head as she laid her hand on his arm. "You can't blame yourself for Mary's death, Tom. The kind of disease she had—"

"I don't blame myself!" If anything, he was more furious. He threw off her hand and lunged to his feet. "I know all about the kind of cancer she had. She only had one choice and she refused to take it. I wanted her to go into the hospital for chemotherapy and the radiation the doctors recommended. But Mary wasn't having any of that."

"You know how she felt about prolonging her illness." She strove for a reasonable tone of voice, glossing over the hurt that had cut deep when he'd tossed her hand off him. "Mary's chances of survival were slim to none. She knew that. She preferred to spend what time she had pursuing as normal a life as she could. For you and the children—"

"But she could have tried to beat it! She didn't have to give up and choose to die!" It was a roar of pain.

"She didn't think she had a choice." How to make him understand Mary had done what she'd done for him? "She chose not to have your last memories of her be filled with months of hospitalization and pain and suffering." She thought back to the last summer of Mary's life, watching her friend grow weaker and more dependent on the pain medications...how could any of them have endured months or years of that?

But Tom wasn't going to be pacified. "She should have let me in on the decision-making," he said bitterly. "It was my life, too."

"Maybe she couldn't. Maybe she knew you couldn't accept it." That was the truth as far as she was concerned. Tom had badgered Mary to see more doctors, over and over again. "I was her friend. She shared her thoughts with me and believe me, her decisions were as painful for her as her death was for you."

"You *were* her friend, weren't you? Why didn't you try to stop her?" It was almost a sneer and she realized with a start that she'd become the focus of his rage. His eyes narrowed and his voice grew darker with fury. "Maybe Mary's illness suited you. You had the hots for me. We both knew it."

Her mouth opened and closed silently in shock. Her fists clenched as rage filled her. As if in a horrible nightmare, she watched her own hand fly up and smack his face and the stinging of her palm as it fell away from his cheek made it all too horribly real.

The flat slap of flesh against flesh echoed in the suddenly silent room.

Shock immediately filled his eyes, followed by dawning awareness and remorse. She realized he'd been so caught up in his rage that perhaps he hadn't been fully aware of what he'd been saying. Still, the pain was too raw, too fresh for her to forgive instantly. The shining beginning of her new marriage lay in shards, forever tarnished, between them.

In a voice barely above a whisper, she said, "I won't let you blame me for something that was no one's fault." She looked him squarely in the eye. "And I may have had the hots for you, but I never tried to get you to forsake your marriage vows for me."

It was cheap, a direct shot fired into the memory of the night that had been unacknowledged between them for so long. She saw it register even as she regretted it. As her anger cooled, she could see what he couldn't—Tom wasn't angry at Mary for not including him in her medical decisions. He was angry at her for dying.

Somehow his grief had gotten sidetracked in rage and until he was able to recognize it and let it go, they didn't have a hope of making their marriage work.

Wearily she turned away, leaving her heart trampled in tiny pieces beneath his feet. "I'm going to bed."

She washed her face and brushed her teeth, then looked in on the children before going into the master bedroom. A sudden moment of indecision assailed her and she paused. Should she sleep in the guest room tonight? Somehow, she couldn't envision facing Tom in bed, having to pretend there was nothing wrong between them. Tomorrow morning in front of the kids would be bad enough.

Tears blurred her vision.

When the door opened suddenly and Tom entered, she turned away, unwilling to show him how much he had hurt her. She could see him in the mirror over the dresser and she schooled her expression into a blank mask. It wasn't his fault that she wasn't the woman he still loved.

He crossed the carpet, moving soundlessly for a big man, and stood behind her. Their gazes met in the mirror. "I don't want to fight with you."

She looked away. "I don't want to fight with you, either."

"Tannis—be patient with me. I want this marriage to work."

She heard the silent apology beneath his halting words, and her heart swelled with love and sympathy. Hurt was forgotten in the overwhelming urge to comfort the man she loved. She would have turned into his arms then, but he put his hands on her shoulders and held her in place. When she looked into the mirror and saw the reflection of his face, a quiver of desire raced through her. He always got that intent, absorbed look on his face when he was making love to her. She craved it because she knew that when he gazed at her body with that open, hungry expression, he wasn't thinking of anyone else but her.

He was looking at her like that now. Just thinking of what he would do hardened her nipples beneath the fabric of her knit shirt and thin bra. She knew the instant he noticed.

One lean hand lifted and settled smoothly, possessively on her breast. The sudden heat and the gentle circling of his thumb around her nipple made her suck in a breath as fire flared in her belly. She glanced in the mirror and was riveted by the sight of his tall frame dwarfing hers, his dark head bent to her neck. He nuzzled her hair aside and placed his lips against the pulse beating at the base of her throat.

She moaned. Again she tried to turn to him, craving front-to-front contact but again he prevented her.

"Wait," he murmured against her neck.

His hands went to the buttons at the neck of her shirt. When he had slipped them open, he seized the bottom of the garment and tugged it free of her pants, then drew it over her head and tossed it aside without ever taking his eyes from her body. She wore only a lacy bra with her trousers now. His hands moved down to her belt, unbuckling and discarding it in the same manner he had her shirt before he slowly unbuttoned the closure of her sport slacks. The hiss of the zipper sliding down its track echoed in her ear; obediently she stepped out of the pants when he tugged them down over her hips.

Almost eagerly her gaze sought the mirror. He was still behind her, looking down over her shoulder at the shape he'd revealed. She could feel his chest rise and fall with increased excitement, and his hot breath seared her flesh. His hands were on her hips, pulling her back against him. They were large and dark against her fair skin. As she watched, he drew them up over the indentation of her waist and slipped them over her ribs until they hovered just beneath her breasts, contained as they were in the champagne lace. One thumb rose and whisked over a taut tip.

Her body jerked in his arms.

He laughed, a deep growl against her neck. "Ah, you like that." Again he repeated the teasing caress, and again, establishing a steady rhythm and joining in with his other thumb at the opposite breast. Between her legs, a wanting began. It increased in intensity until she began to shift her hips slightly back and forth in a vain attempt to find some relief.

She was still watching when one finger unfurled and hooked in the fabric of her bra, and she moaned and threw her head back against his shoulder when the rosy crest was exposed. Immediately his hand covered it, shaping and circling, tormenting. He repeated the process with the other breast, and she raised her head again.

It was an incredibly erotic sight. He stood behind her fully clothed. Her nearly naked body gleamed in the lamplight. His hands played at her bared breasts and her breath whistled in and out as she felt the first stirrings of a damp blossoming uncurl between her legs.

As if he knew what she was feeling, his left hand ceased its mastery of her breast and made a leisurely foray down her torso, over her navel, over the flat plane of her belly. In the mirror, she watched him delve beneath the lacy edging of her panties and comb his fingers through the triangle of red curls he found there. But he didn't linger. Both hands left her body and she almost cried out, to beg him not to stop. Then her dazed senses registered a new freedom as he deftly unhooked the back clasp of her bra and drew it away, and then inserted his thumbs in the lacy panties and pulled them off, as well.

She felt wild and abandoned, looking at herself naked in the mirror. When he came into focus beside her, she saw he'd removed his clothes as well. He was aroused, powerfully so and the sight of his bold male flesh caused a fresh ache in her loins.

He stepped behind her again. Taking her by the hips, he pulled her up and back against him and she could feel the long, hot length of him pressed against her. She wriggled her bottom against him and he groaned as his sensitive man's flesh nestled in the crevice of her buttocks. Reflexively he rocked his hips against her. One hand slid around to claim the tender flesh of her inner thigh and she relaxed, widening her legs in invitation, uncaring of the picture she presented.

Tom grimaced, a wild baring of his teeth as he let her slip down to the floor again. "Watch."

One hand claimed her breast again while the other slipped more intimately between her legs. As she watched in the mirror in helpless arousal, he touched her, touched her, touched her with smooth circles and steady pressure and sweet forays into her damp heat, touched her until her body caught fire. Ecstasy raced through her like wildfire in a dry forest. She bucked and arched against his hands while he continued to play her, wringing every small response from her until she was breathless and gasping in his arms.

With the last of her strength, she pulled his hands away. "No more. Please."

He chuckled, little more than a growl in his chest. "Yes. More."

He pressed her forward, bending her at the waist and positioning her limp arms on the wide bureau before her. Behind her, he bent and grasped one of her ankles, widening her stance. Then, before she fully understood what he was about to do, he grasped her hips and moved against her—satiny, slippery strength against softness. He paused for a moment, then tilted his hips forward and firmly filled her, wringing a startled cry from her. Immediately he began a driving, demanding dance of passion.

She couldn't have stood alone, could barely hang on to reality as she bent over the dresser and he measured her receptiveness again and again. He slid one hand around her to brace against her belly, the other one again slipped down to the slick heat between her thighs. She moaned, unable to take the intensity of feeling his touch produced. The world darkened for a moment.

Through his teeth he muttered again, "Watch," and she looked up, into the mirror. His jaw was clenched, his eyes blazed. She felt his body kick into a final frantic finish and suddenly, a well of unsuspected heat flashed through her again and she convulsed around him.

He carried her to bed afterward, and in the middle of the night, when he reached for her and pulled her beneath him, she responded with all the love she carried in her heart for this man who wouldn't accept anything more than her body.

And Mary still stood between them.

Eight

Amy came bouncing in from the family room to greet him the next evening when he brought Jeb home from ball practice just in time for dinner. He glanced over her head but Tannis didn't appear.

"Daddy, you promised tonight we'd talk about me staying home," Amy reminded him.

Her big eyes were both hopeful and wary. They were so like her mother's that he had a sudden, vivid image of Mary standing before him. He automatically braced for the stab of pain that usually accompanied thoughts of her, but strangely, it didn't tear into him as before. The smile he gave his daughter was bright in contrast. "We will. How about right after supper when Jebbie will probably go out to play with his friends?"

"Great!" Amy's hair was loose around her shoulders today; it danced from side to side as she turned away.

"Where's Tannis?"

"In the kitchen. She's teaching me how to bake fish fillets."

As Amy headed back to the kitchen, Tom draped his jacket over the hall post. He eyed the empty hallway to the kitchen speculatively. This was the first night Tannis hadn't greeted him at the door since they'd married. When he'd woken in the morning, he'd done his best to act normal and forget the ugly scene he'd created last night, but she still must be annoyed.

Well, hell. He'd been a jerk. He knew it. He couldn't talk about Mary without anger rising and grabbing him by the throat, and for some stupid reason he'd taken it out on Tannis. He hadn't been fair. Afterward, he'd tried to show her how much she meant to him, but apparently she hadn't gotten the message.

In the kitchen, she looked up from her work at the counter and smiled. Her face was full of the usual warm welcome she extended to him. "Hi."

"Hi." He rounded the corner of the breakfast bar and bent to kiss her tentatively. He almost expected that she'd turn away, but to his surprise she leaned into him with a quiet murmur of pleasure that sent immediate signals of sweet stirring response through his loins. He was so relieved that she wasn't still mad about last night that he let himself go with sensation, totally forgetting Amy's presence in the room. God, he wanted her! He loved his kids, but this was one of those times when he'd give a lot to be alone with his wife.

He deepened the kiss, seeking her tongue and growling deep in his throat at the open, easy way she offered herself to him. She curled her body into his, offering him all the devotion and love a man could wish for—

Love?

The thought shocked him enough that he released her and stepped away, mumbling something lame about reminding Jeb to wash his hands before dinner. As he escaped up the stairs, he allowed himself to think again of Tannis.

And love. On reflection, the idea rather appealed to him. Did she love him? She certainly acted as if she did. No one looking at their recent marriage would suspect the unorthodox proposal that had prompted it. So...was she just playacting to fend off the questions?

No, that didn't make sense. If that were the case, she would treat him with a public facade, but she wouldn't bother to extend it in private, unless she was only doing it to convince the kids...and the enthusiasm with which she responded to his every caress was overkill, in that case.

One day last week, she'd massaged his shoulders when he'd come home after a rare day in court. He'd been tense and distracted by the case in which he was involved, a case in which his deceased elderly client's son and daughter hadn't even waited until after the funeral to begin fighting for control of the considerable estate. It was nothing he hadn't seen before, but he doubted he'd ever get used to the avariciousness

and greed relatives so often displayed when there was
money at stake.

He'd never talked much about his work to Mary.
But with Tannis, something was different. She showed
interest, compassion, concern. She made him feel as
if his problems were important to her. As if *he* were
important to her.

Immediately he mentally drew back from the dis-
loyal thought. He'd been important to Mary, too. Her
way had been different. She was so involved in her
hundred-and-one community projects that he'd never
quite felt she was really hearing him when he tried to
talk to her about his work, but she'd supported him
just the same. And she'd loved him.

And that brought him back full circle to his origi-
nal line of thinking. The more he thought about it, the
more sure he became that Tannis loved him. All the
little special touches she'd brought into his life were
signposts indicating a deeper feeling.

The knowledge gave him a warm feeling inside, a
contented security that he hadn't realized he'd been
longing for until he had it.

When she came to call him for dinner, he took her
hand and held her beside him as he rose to his feet.
"Maybe we can turn off the TV and talk tonight after
the kids are in bed."

"Talk about what?" She looked a little puzzled.

He shrugged. "Trade childhood memories, anything you like. It occurred to me that I don't know
nearly enough about the woman I married." He could
see he'd pleased her—her fair skin flushed and her
eyes glowed with happiness.

"Maybe we could conduct this conversation in the hot tub," she said, and her voice carried a flirtatious note.

He laughed, putting his hands at her waist and pulling her against him. "If I get in the hot tub with you, I'm going to find it hard to keep my mind on conversation."

"That's what I'm counting on," she whispered as she lifted herself on tiptoe to meet his lips.

He liked it, he decided as he took his seat across from his wife at dinner a few moments later. Being loved by Tannis was a bonus he hadn't expected when he'd decided to marry her, but one for which he'd always be grateful.

A few hours later, when the sounds of a busy household had fallen quiet in slumber, he lay half on her in their big bed, his body replete with the satisfaction that followed total release. Beneath him, Tannis stirred. One hand came up and she combed through his hair with spread fingers, gently scratching his scalp with her nails.

He sighed with pleasure and shifted off her, gathering her into his arms. "You've changed my life in so many good ways."

He felt her smile against his chest. "You'll excuse me if I find that statement slightly suspect. After what we just did in this bed—"

"And in the hot tub," he reminded her smugly.

"And in the hot tub. I think your point of view might be a little biased."

He rolled her onto her back, looking down into her wide blue eyes. "I mean it. Having you in my bed is my private fantasy come true, but having you in my life has been good for all of us." He shifted back a pace. "Thank you for helping me talk to Amy tonight. I have to begin to trust her in small ways, to realize that she's maturing and needs some independence. Why couldn't I figure that out before?"

"Maybe you were too caught up in trying to keep the kids' lives as normal as possible to see the need for any changes."

"That's probably true. Now I know why I married you," he teased.

"I already know." She moved out of his arms and turned her back on him, clasping her pillow beneath her head as if it were necessary for survival. "We're good in bed together, and I'm a help with the children."

It caught him so off guard that he merely lay there. One minute she'd been in his arms, sharing quiet after-loving conversation; the next, she was giving him a definite cold shoulder. Did she really expect him to accept that she was going to sleep that way all night, with her back to him? Hell, she'd slept in his arms every night since he'd married her.

Her words began to penetrate. Was that really what she thought? That he had married her *only* because he liked the sex between them and because she was good with Amy and Jeb?

Then it hit him.

Of course that was what she thought. That *was* why he'd married her. Wasn't it? Uncomfortably he shifted. He hated being forced to examine his actions, but he had to be honest with her and with him-

self. He'd married her because...because at some
subconscious level, he must have recognized her love.
Because he needed her. Needed her to love him, to
soothe the rough edges of his days and stimulate his
body to senseless fulfillment every night.

Placing his hand on her shoulder, he rolled her back
toward him, pinning her neatly by placing his body
atop hers again.

"Tom!" She squirmed, but he noticed in the
moonlight coming through the window that she
wouldn't look him in the eye. "I need to get to sleep.
I have to work tomorrow."

"So do I. But I can't sleep with misunderstanding
between us." He put a hand up and cupped her chin,
holding her so he could see her face. Was that hurt he
saw in her gaze? He bent his head and set his lips to
hers, kissing her gently, skillfully, with all the tender
feeling she aroused in him until the stiffness left her
body and she was kissing him back.

"Do you love me?" he muttered against her lips.

Her body stilled for an instant, then stiffened again.
"Wha—"

"Tell me you love me." He resumed the heated
kisses, slipping his hand down to shape the warm
mound of her breast, and she squeaked in protest or
response. He wasn't sure which, but he couldn't stop
now. "I want to hear you say it. Add to your list of
reasons for our marriage that I needed your love. And
I'll take good care of it, I promise you."

Slowly her body relaxed beneath his. He drew away
for a minute and an expectant silence fell.

She brought her hands up and placed them on his
cheeks, looking straight into his eyes. "I love you,

Tom," she said softly. "I've loved you for a long time."

Jubilation exploded within him. "I knew it." His voice caught and he had to clear his throat, burying his lips in her hair and pulling her as close as he could. "My red-haired enchantress. Do you have any idea how much I need you?"

Easter passed. Her mother's doctor talked Madeline into having the tests of which they'd spoken. He recommended a new medication and after it was administered, Tannis was startled at the change in her mother—the troubling aggressiveness diminished markedly.

Tom went with her faithfully to visit Madeline every week and Tannis watched him handle her with amused resignation. Why had she thought any woman would be able to withstand a concentrated dose of the Hayes charm?

As their marriage neared the three-month mark, their lives fell into a pattern. She'd never dreamed that marriage to Tom could make her so happy. He was considerate and thoughtful, bringing her flowers and small gifts every time she blinked. He took seriously her opinions about child-rearing and frequently sought her advice and he began to *listen* to her. And he was so helpful around the house that she felt none of the kind of pressure that had plagued her self-esteem in her first marriage.

Even the memory of his early, hurtful comment about not marrying her for her housekeeping skills faded, because she began to realize that he truly hadn't meant it as a slur. Tom's life revolved around his family and a fanatically tidy house was well down on the list of things about which he cared.

And then there was the lovemaking. She'd begun to think of it that way because he took such clear pleasure in hearing her voice her love for him. The night on which he'd forced her confession had been a turning point in their relationship. Now that she felt free to express her love, she did so at every opportunity.

And if it bothered her just the teeniest bit that he had yet to respond in kind, she shrugged it off. Tom cared for her, of that she was sure. So what if he couldn't say the words yet?

Yet. That was what she lived for, what was keeping her going. She'd become his partner in everything else that affected their lives, and she was banking on the hope that one day he'd be able to say goodbye to Mary in his heart. Or at least allow her to slide aside far enough to allow Tannis in as well.

She came out of her reverie as her students began to file in from afternoon recess. The laughing, chattering crowd of fourth-graders was hard to reach these days, with the late May sunshine pouring in through the windows and the warm spring breezes swirling across the playground. She asked them to take out their science notebooks, but as she walked around the room encouraging and challenging, a figure in the doorway attracted her attention. It was Mr. Tenlow, the principal.

"You're needed in the office," he said. "I'll take your class."

"What's wrong?" Automatically she handed him the checklist she'd been using to gauge her students' progress on the team observation projects in which they were engaged.

"Amy isn't feeling well. She's asking for you."

As soon as she'd briefed him on what the class was to do in her absence, Tannis walked rapidly to the office.

The school's secretary met her in the outer office before she could charge into the health room. "Can I talk to you before you go in to Amy?" Janine wore many hats when the itinerant nurses and counselors weren't in the building. Apparently she'd been with Amy.

"Sure, what's wrong?"

Janine led Tannis into the principal's office and closed the door. "I've been talking to Amy, but I called you up here because I can't do a thing with her."

"Why? Is she sick? Maybe I should call Tom."

"No!" Janine shook her head. "That's exactly the problem. Amy started her menstrual period in class today."

"Oh." For once, Tannis was at a loss. Hadn't anyone prepared Amy for the changes her body would be going through? Even if Tom hadn't, she knew the school had a two-day seminar conducted during the fifth-grade health classes in the spring. Surely Amy had participated in those last year. "Didn't she understand what was happening?"

"Oh, yes," the secretary assured her. "She was a little concerned, as all young girls are at first, but she knew what to expect."

Tannis spread her hands in question. "Well then, I don't see what the problem is."

Janine raked an exasperated hand through her steel gray curls. "The problem, Tannis, is your husband."

"My husband...?"

"Ever since his first wife died, Mr. Hayes has been...shall we say, overly concerned about his children's health. Every time one of them sniffles, he races them to the doctor."

Tannis almost smiled. "Yes, he does have a bit of a phobia about illness, but what does that have to do with Amy's current situation?"

"Mr. Tenlow remembered you had two parent conferences scheduled after school today, and he thought perhaps her father's schedule might be a bit more flexible. But when I told Amy I was going to call her dad, Amy got...well, almost hysterical. She begged us not to call him and she got more and more upset, to the point that she wants you and only you."

"I see." She really didn't, but now that she knew Amy needed her, she could find out the rest. "May I talk to her privately?"

Janine breathed a sigh of relief. "Be my guest." She opened the door of the office. "She's in the health room."

Tannis made her way to the other room, cautiously opening the door. "Amy? Honey, it's me. Can I come in?"

"Tannis!" Amy's pretty face was tear-streaked and blotchy. She threw herself into Tannis's arms and sobbed as if her heart were broken.

Thinking back to the turbulent emotions that had dominated her own adolescence, Tannis figured Amy probably felt that way right now. This was a time of big change in a young girl's life. Puberty might magnify the grief Amy still felt at her mother's death and create some pretty big mountains out of minor mole-hills. Gently she stroked the ponytail that had lost its usual sprightly lilt and rubbed Amy's back.

"Would it help to talk about it, honey?"

The girl lifted her face from Tannis's shoulder. "Please don't let them call Daddy!"

Her plea was so fervent that Tannis was taken aback. "I'm here now," she hedged, unwilling to make such a promise until she knew exactly what was wrong. "Tell me what's the matter. Mrs. McDowell told me you got...you just began your first menstrual cycle."

Amy sniffed and nodded. "But that's not why I didn't want them to call Daddy." She sat up and looked at Tannis. "I'm not the first girl in my class to start my period. Other people's moms just take them home and show them what to do—to take care of it, I mean." Her face reddened slightly, but she plowed on. "Tannis, you know Daddy. If he takes me out of school, you *know* what he'll do. He'll make me go to the doctor. *Nobody else* has to go to the doctor," she wailed. "I'll be *so* embarrassed."

She wanted to defend Tom, but she knew Amy had him pegged. He *would* drag her right off to the doctor. Desperately, she tried for diplomacy. "Amy, you realize it's a good idea to visit a doctor after you begin to menstruate. Most girls' parents do take them to visit a physician sometime after that first period occurs."

Amy pounced on that. "Yeah, but not *ten minutes* after. Please, Tannis, don't make me call him."

"I won't." She didn't feel that was an unreasonable promise to make. "But you agree that we'll tell him tonight?"

"Sure."

"Uh, Amy?"

"Yeah?"

"Do you need anything? I mean, would you like me to help you get comfortable with the things you need to do now?"

Amy's eyes filled again. "I want to go home. I ruined my underwear, and I only have this little pack of stuff the nurse gave me and would you go to the store and get me some—"

"Shhh." Tannis put her arm around her stepdaughter. "Let me finish my science class and get my students on the bus. Then I'll take you home and we'll run by the store on the way. Okay?" She tilted Amy's chin up and was relieved to see a watery smile.

"Okay."

Tannis rose from the side of the divan where they'd been sitting. She smoothed her hand over Amy's hair one last time. "You rest here and I'll bring your things from your class after the last bell rings."

Less than an hour later, she pulled into the driveway with Amy, Jeb and a bag of feminine hygiene items she'd purchased. While Jeb did his homework, she helped Amy figure out what to use and washed out the soiled undergarments. A chat to find out exactly what Amy knew and needed to understand about her body might be prudent ... Tannis sighed. Sixth-grade seemed so young to be starting on sexual enlightenment! She'd have to handle the whole issue very carefully.

The rest of the afternoon passed quickly. Jeb finished his homework and asked for permission to play outside. Amy lay on the sofa, and as he passed her, he looked at her curiously.

"Hey! Whatsa matter with Amy? Did she throw up?" He looked so avidly interested that Tannis had to chuckle.

"No, nothing like that." She almost laughed again at the disappointment on his face. "She just isn't feeling well."

"Man, I bet Daddy lets her stay home from school tomorrow," he said. But in the next instant, his disgust was gone. "I'm going out to play ball with Miles," he hollered bare seconds before the sliding door to the deck slid forcefully shut.

Tannis lowered her papers and exchanged a wry glance with Amy. "Don't slam the door," she said, and Amy dissolved into giggles.

She stuffed a chicken and put it in to bake. Closer to dinnertime, she prepared a fruit salad, mixed biscuits and started a cheese sauce to drizzle over the broccoli. Funny how much she enjoyed the evening ritual of preparing a meal to feed her family. Her culinary skill was the one thing Jeremy had rarely criticized, but after the divorce she'd lumped cooking in with all the other housekeeping duties at which she felt inadequate.

Amy seemed to recover and came in to help set the table, chattering a mile a minute about the cheerleading tryouts for next year she hoped to participate in the following week. Jeb came back in from playing ball.

"Something smells good." He flipped on the oven light. "I love chicken." Then he strained on tiptoe to see what she was doing at the sink. "Broccoli. Oh, yuck. I can't stand broccoli."

"If you can't say something polite, don't say it at all," Tannis informed him with a smile to soften the words. "Go wash your hands. We'll eat as soon as your father gets here."

Just as Jeb turned away from the sink, the front door opened.

"Dad!" Jeb made a beeline for the door. "I caught four flies in a row when I was playing catch with Miles this afternoon."

Tannis heard Tom's deep voice, soft with affection. "Way to go, buddy. Wish I could have seen that."

"I gotta wash my hands. We're almost ready to eat. Dad, Amy got sick at school today. Will she be able to eat with us?"

"Amy got sick—?"

Tannis heard Tom's footsteps, rapid and urgent, an instant before he burst into the kitchen. Instead of the usual intimate smile with which he greeted her, his face was dark and boiling with anger, like the sky in the last moments before a violent storm. He made no effort to kiss her.

"Where's Amy? What's wrong with her?"

Tannis hesitated, pointing. What was wrong with *him?* He looked furious, but she had no idea why.

Amy came around the corner from the dining room. "Hi, Daddy. Gotta go wash my hands." She casually stretched up to kiss Tom's jaw. Then, before either of them could react, she sashayed out of the room, and they heard the bathroom door close.

"What is going on here? Jeb said Amy was sick." Tom's voice was low and controlled but Tannis could still see rage leaping beneath the surface.

She spread her hands in unconscious appeal. "Amy's probably a little shy about telling you herself." She allowed a small smile to tilt her lips. "Your little girl isn't a little girl anymore. She started her period today."

"She started..." Tom looked stunned, but it passed in a heartbeat, and his brows lowered again. "Is everything okay? What did the doctor say?"

"I haven't taken her to the doctor yet. It's not necessary. I thought we should wait until Amy gets through this first time before we make an appointment." She swallowed nervously. It made perfect sense to her, but Tom didn't appear to be placated.

"It's not necessary? What the hell does that mean?" he yelled.

Tannis was shocked by his sudden loss of control. "Tom, I—I didn't think—"

"You didn't think? You obviously thought long enough to decide to exclude me from knowing about my own daughter's health." He wasn't yelling anymore, but the icy venom in his tone spread through her system like a toxic dose of poison. "Let me tell you something, *Mrs. Hayes*. You may bear the same last name as my children do now, but that doesn't give you the right to make decisions concerning them. These are *my* children. All decisions made regarding their health and welfare will be made by *me*."

Her voice shook with her distress. "But, Tom, Amy's not sick. I didn't believe this was—"

"You have no rights, do you hear me? No right at all. Don't you *ever* presume you know what's best for my children without consulting me. Is that clear?"

Oh, it was clear, all right. Her heart had shrunken into a small, frozen ball of ice in her breast. At first, she'd felt guilty, as if she were the one at fault, as if she'd made some terribly erroneous assumption that had jeopardized Amy's life. But almost as quickly as the thought came, she'd rejected it.

Never again was a man going to drive her self-worth out the window and replace it with cowering indecision and an ego the size of the head of a pin. Rage flowered and burst into red-hot life.

"Do you realize how crazy you sound?" Her own voice was strident and angry, but she didn't care. "Every time somebody around here gets so much as a sniffle, you're dragging them off to the doctor. Do you know why I didn't call you?" She stepped closer and poked a finger rigid with rage into his chest. "Because Amy didn't want me to. Your own daughter begged me not to call you because she knew this is exactly how you'd react. If your own children can see how irrational your behavior is, why can't you?"

"I don't care how crazy you think I seem. No one in my family is going to suffer from a lack of medical care if I can help it. Not Amy, not Jeb and not you."

Dimly Tannis realized they would regret these harsh, hateful words forever, that she should simply walk away from him, but she was too wrapped up in expressing her anger to watch her words. "You know what the real problem here is, Tom? You're still punishing Mary. Well, *I'm not Mary!* And I'm getting darn sick and tired of trying to prove it. Mary is really the one you're mad at because she didn't do what you thought she should. Mary made the best decision for *her* that she could, and she believed it was the best thing she could do for all of you. Face facts, Tom. Mary was terminally ill and she knew it! She didn't want the end of her life to be ugly and undignified, to drag on and on until all of us prayed for the pain and suffering to end—"

"Just shut up!" Tom pushed his face close to hers and it was twisted and ugly with rage. "You don't know what you're talking about." He spun away from her and slammed a fist against the door to the basement. There was a crashing, shattering sound as his fist drove through the wood.

Silence descended in the kitchen.

Tom stood frozen for a moment, then his gaze swung away from the sight of the hole he'd made in the door and his green eyes narrowed as they focused on her. He reached out a hand.

She took a step back, away from Tom. Her hands were over her mouth, but she didn't remember putting them there.

Sudden awareness flared in his gaze. He took a deep breath and she could almost see him relaxing his muscles one by one.

"Tannis, don't you know I'd never hurt you?" His voice was soft and gentle and all traces of the fury of a moment before seemed to have vanished.

For the first time, she noticed his hand. The knuckles were scraped and bleeding and there were several long, ugly scratches running the length of his forearm where he'd unthinkingly pulled it free of the wood.

Turning from him, she silently went to the cupboard and pulled out a bottle of antiseptic cleaner. Then she took an ice pack out of the refrigerator and slipped it into a clean, soft fabric cover. She set it on the counter beside the antiseptic. "You'd better clean that and put some ice on it." Her voice sounded strange to her ears.

Tom moved toward her and again she stepped back.

He halted. "Honey, I won't hurt you." His features twisted a moment in something like pain. "I promise."

His gentle tone almost melted the protective layer of ice in which she'd encased her emotions. Tears threatened. She swallowed, then said slowly, "You promised to love, honor and cherish also, and you've done none of those."

His chest expanded as he drew breath to speak, but she cut him off.

"This marriage was a mistake. I love you, Tom. I guess I thought I could heal you, even make you love again. But I can't watch you destroy yourself and your children with your obsessive kind of love."

The words fell into the silence with the shattering finality of a twenty-one-gun salute. Unable to bear looking at his beloved face any longer, afraid she'd beg for the unattainable if she stayed, she turned and quietly went through the house to the front door.

Nine

What had he done?

The quiet click of the front door as she left mocked him. Tom shook his head slowly, like a man orienting himself after a particularly vicious nightmare. A sudden tingle of pain caused him to raise his hand and inspect it.

Wow. He flexed his fingers and cursed vividly at the agony that shot through his mangled fist. The knuckles were already turning deep, muted shades of purple and blue. He'd be damned lucky if he hadn't broken a few.

He shook his head again, ruefully this time, but there was no humor in it. He couldn't remember feeling that sense of uncontrollable exploding rage ever before in his life, not even when Mary got sick. What the hell had gotten into him?

Mary is really the one you're mad at.

God, was she right? Had this anger been festering inside him since Mary's death? He was almost afraid to admit it could be so.

He walked to the sink and leaned on its edge, turning the water on as hot as he could stand it before he thrust his hand and arm under the cleansing flow. He winced and swore again, gingerly soaping and rinsing it as the pain returned with a nasty jolt, and before he could chicken out, he quickly poured antiseptic over the wounds, gritting his teeth against the stinging pain. It was a real relief to pick up the ice pack and cradle it against his swollen hand.

Where had Tannis gone? She couldn't have left for good. Could she? The first icy tendrils of real fear crawled through his gut. She hadn't even taken car keys. She'd have to come back.

But what would that matter? After the way he'd treated her, she'd be more than justified if she tossed him out of her life like some piece of rotting meat.

And that's what he guessed he'd been doing. Rotting inside.

You selfish, stupid, S.O.B. It seemed so pointless now, to be harboring anger at Mary for not choosing to accept his wishes regarding her medical treatment. Tannis was right. Mary had deserved his full support for her decisions about her life, and she hadn't gotten it.

And to make matters worse, he'd gotten lucky enough to marry a second woman who loved him, loved him despite his flaws, and he'd failed to support her, either.

If Tannis was reading him right—and he reluctantly admitted that every word she'd thrown at him had fit like a well-broken-in-shoe—he'd transferred all his fury at Mary into a more acceptable, but equally destructive, channel by worrying himself to pieces over the health of his remaining family. Almost as if he were thumbing his nose at Mary.

Ha-ha. See? You might have left me, but I'm not going to let anybody else do it.

Come to think of it, that's exactly how he'd felt. As if in defying illness he was cheating *Mary* of something. How stupid he'd been. He couldn't cheat Mary. She was gone. And if he were honest, he was glad of the way she'd gone relatively pain-free, slipping quietly into death one Sunday morning only weeks after she'd become too ill to leave her bed.

At the time, he hadn't appreciated the ease with which she'd passed away. As he'd watched her loving eyes dim, he'd nursed rage in his heart, dreamt of revenge. His own twisted revenge, incomprehensible and meaningless to anyone else.

Except someone who loved him.

Someone like Tannis. She'd fallen in love with him just as he was, warts and all. And now he found he was shedding some of those warts. God, it was good to let go of the past!

He felt cleansed and renewed. Why hadn't he recognized his grief? For that was exactly what it had been, a part of his grieving for Mary. And until he faced it and released it, there'd been no chance that this new marriage could work.

But it could now.

If only he could get Tannis to give him another chance. That door had shut behind her with an ominous finality. Even if she walked through it now, he knew she wouldn't be staying. Unless—

"Daddy?"

Tom whirled.

Jeez, he'd completely forgotten about Amy and Jeb. They stood together in the hallway just outside the kitchen. Amy had her hands on Jeb's shoulders in a protective gesture, but her young face looked frightened.

"Hey, guys." Tom tried a reassuring smile. "Come on in."

Neither child moved.

"Where's Tannis?" asked Jeb.

Tom sighed. "I think she went for a walk. We had a big fight, and I hurt her feelings." He raised his injured hand. "I get the prize for being the Boob of the Year."

Jeb giggled. Both children advanced into the kitchen to inspect his hand, and his son's eyes widened at the sight of the hole in the door. "That wasn't too bright, Dad," he pronounced.

"You can say that again. Think you could give me some lessons on how to handle angry feelings in a better way?"

Amy smirked. "Mom used to tell me to punch a pillow. Guess you should do that, too."

Tom raised a hand to her cheek as she smiled fully at him. "Thanks, Ame. I'll try that next time."

"I hope there isn't a next time." Jeb's young voice was vehement. "It scared me when you and Tannis started to fight."

"There won't be." Tom knew he could make that promise with genuine commitment. "If Tannis forgives me for this, I'm never going to shout at her again. Argue with her, maybe, but not shout."

"Daddy?" Nerves showed in Amy's eyes, but so did a trace of the defiance, which was so familiar these days. "I heard what you two were saying. It's my fault Tannis didn't tell you about my—sickness—I asked her not to. If you want to be mad at somebody, you should be mad at me."

"I'm not mad at anybody, Amy. I—"

"Daddy, you embarrass us when you make us go to the doctor every time some little thing happens. Why can't we be like other kids and only go once a year unless we get really, really sick?"

Amy's voice had risen in agitation and Tom stared at her. "You never told me you felt this way before."

She rolled her eyes. "I knew you'd just ignore me."

"I won't ignore your feelings anymore," he said quietly, knowing he deserved her response. "I think you and Tannis are right. I have been worrying too much about your health. From now on the people in this household will only go to the doctor for regular yearly checkups."

"Unless they get really, really sick or hurt," Amy added with a delighted smile.

"Right." He smiled back at her, then turned his attention to Jeb, who still was looking troubled. "What's the matter, buddy?" He tried not to wince, holding his injured hand out of the way as Jeb climbed into his arms.

"Dad, is Tannis going to leave us forever, like Mommy did?"

The innocent question cut him to the quick. And the ice congealed in his stomach again. "I don't know, Jeb." He couldn't be less than truthful with his children. "I upset her pretty badly earlier—"

"But I want her to stay! I love Tannis." Fat tears began to roll down Jeb's cheeks and he buried his face in Tom's shirt.

"I know." Tom rubbed his back in circles just as he'd done when Jeb was a small, fussy baby. *I love Tannis.* The words echoed between them, and a great warmth swelled in his chest.

I love her, too. How could he have refused to see it for so long? He couldn't resist trying it aloud.

"I love her, too, and I want her to stay." It sounded good. No, it sounded great! He couldn't wait for her to return to apologize, to ask her for another chance and tell her how much he loved her. He had to go to her *now*.

Inspiration struck as the smell of cooking chicken suddenly penetrated his preoccupied senses. He tried to make his request sound as normal as possible. "Amy, could you get dinner on the table while I go find Tannis? I want to talk to her alone before we eat."

Amy brightened and he could almost see her puffing up with importance. "Sure, Daddy." She held out her hand to Jeb and he could have kissed her for that small, thoughtful gesture. "Come on, Jebbie. You can help me put the sauce on the broccoli and get the drinks."

Tannis was coming up the path from the little lake at the bottom of their development when she saw Tom striding toward her. Instantly her shoulders stiffened defensively. Oh, she knew he'd never hit her, never hurt her physically, but her ego didn't need any more cruel words.

He couldn't know how deeply his repudiation of her had hurt. All her life she'd wanted to belong, to be a part of a true partnership. And even though he'd never said he'd loved her, with Tom she'd felt as if finally she had found her niche. They'd formed a partnership. She'd thought they were a unit, making mutual decisions for the family she had easily accepted in her heart.

But Tom hadn't looked at it that way. As she'd found when she overstepped the invisible boundary of responsibility today, he didn't regard her input as anything more than a courtesy.

Maybe he never would. Maybe she couldn't heal him. She'd realized he was still caught up in part of his grieving, that he had yet to reach the stage of the healing process the experts called Acceptance. When she'd walked out the front door twenty minutes earlier, she'd thought her marriage was over. Her heart was ripped into several small pieces, her feelings lacerated and bleeding. But as she'd walked—and cried— she'd realized she couldn't give up on Tom Hayes.

Funny, she never thought she'd be thanking Jeremy for anything, but it was because of him that she'd reached down into herself and found inner strength, the strength that she would need if she was ever going to reach Tom.

As she watched his long legs eat up the distance between them, and the late-day sun shining on his dark hair, her heart felt as if it would burst with love.

And pain. What if he didn't want to try again? What if he'd taken her seriously? In her heart she couldn't regret her actions of the day. Amy had needed *her*, not a doctor. There was nothing wrong with her judgment.

She set her teeth as he neared her, and she could see the unsmiling line of his strong jaw. If he lit into her again, she'd fight fire with fire until he'd listen to reason. She wasn't giving up on him. Oh, no. Maybe he had some valid grounds for his feelings, given what he'd been through when Mary was ill. She'd talk to him, and listen, and be there with her love. Even if he could never say the words, she wanted him to know the security of being loved and cared for, of knowing she would never leave. She'd—

"Oh, your poor hand!" The sight of the sullen, oozing raw scratches drove all thoughts of their disagreement out of her head. "Have you called the doctor? Maybe you'd better get that X-rayed."

He came to a halt in front of her, and she was surprised to see what almost looked like a gleam of amusement in his green gaze. "Seems to me those are the words that caused us all the trouble in the first place."

His voice sounded relaxed and definitely mildly amused. She searched his face, confused now. What had happened to the angry man she'd left in the house? Striving for a light tone to match his, she said, "Maybe we should ban the word *d-o-c-t-o-r* from our house."

Tom's expression sobered immediately and his eyes grew shuttered. "Is it still?"

"Still what?"

"*Our* house. I had the distinct impression you were throwing in the towel when you walked out of it."

Again she searched his face, but it was expressionless now except for a telltale muscle twitching in his right cheek. Baldly she asked, "Do you want it to be ours?" then held her breath.

Something unreadable flickered in his eyes. He hesitated, and she had the fleeting impression he was nervous. She dismissed it immediately. Tom had nerves of tempered steel. Then, to her utter shock, he opened his arms. "Tannis, please come home. I need you."

Joy made the evening sun as bright as a summer day at noon. She took the single step forward that would bring her into his embrace and wrapped her arms around his middle, resting her head in its familiar hollow at his shoulder. Tears stung her eyes. He still hadn't said he loved her, and they hadn't discussed the problems that still stood between them, but *he wanted her to stay!* She lifted her face, offering her mouth for his kiss.

Tom gathered her even closer with his undamaged arm, heedless of the fact that they were standing in the middle of a dead-end residential street. He took her mouth with an intense, sweet wildness that curled her toes and had her clinging to his shoulders. Then, with atypical diffidence, he asked, "Is that a 'yes'?"

She laughed through the tears that were stinging her eyes. "That's a 'yes.'"

He sucked in his breath, and she read the brief spasm of pain that crossed his features. Her heart sank. Was he thinking of Mary even now?

Then he spoke. "I don't deserve you. And you were right earlier. I haven't lived up to my marriage vows."

"Tom, I was angry. I didn't mean—"

He shushed her with a gentle finger touching her lips. "I love you, Tannis Hayes. I should have told you before, but I didn't really understand it until I thought I might lose you. If you'll come home to stay, I'll honor and cherish you as well, every day for the rest of our lives. I've been wrong about the doctor visits and I needed you to make me see it. You've opened up communication between Amy and me, you've become a real mother in my children's hearts. And you've healed me."

"You healed yourself." She was crying freely, too stunned to control her emotions. *Tom loved her!* And it sounded as if he'd come to terms with his past, enough to be able to finally let it go. "All I did was believe in you."

He drew her close again, wiping her cheeks with a big hand and tilting her chin up for his kiss. "Don't ever stop believing in me. Love me always."

"Always," she pledged as his mouth descended.

His kiss was hungry and demanding, filled with the love they shared. When he lifted his head, he heaved a sigh of regret. "Do you think we could get away with skipping dinner?"

"Dinner!" She stared at him for a shocked moment, then pulled out of his arms and started to hurry up the street. "I forgot! We'll be lucky if the house doesn't burn down."

"Relax." He caught her by the waist, cuddling her against his side, and she automatically slowed her pace to match his. "Amy has everything under control. I told the kids I loved you, and that I was coming to get you."

She stopped in the middle of the street, smiling sheepishly when he reached out and closed her open mouth. "You told the kids you loved me?"

He nodded. "And since we can't do anything more exciting than talking about it until after they're in bed, why don't we make a date right now for the hot tub, ten o'clock, tonight?"

"Sounds to me like you're planning on doing a little more than talk." Her voice was warm with anticipation and fond memory.

"Oh, yeah, almost forgot." He gathered her in for a last kiss as they entered the driveway. "You won't need a suit."

Epilogue

It had been the happiest Christmas she'd ever known.

Wincing in discomfort, Tannis tried to find a more comfortable position in the rocking chair Tom had bought her for Christmas. On the floor, Tom and Jeb were flat on their stomachs beneath the softly lit Christmas tree, rearranging the model train set to accommodate the new pieces of landscape that Jeb had received.

Stacks of opened presents and wadded-up balls of discarded gift wrap decorated every available surface.

Amy lounged on the sofa, chewing bubblegum which she cracked periodically as she avidly turned the pages of *Little Women*. It was one of a set of classics Tannis had given her earlier in the day.

Tannis felt her eyelids closing despite the persistent dull pain in her abdomen. It had been a big day. After opening their gifts at the crack of dawn when Jeb roused them all, they'd driven up to Culpeper and taken her mother out to a restaurant. An hour-long drive each way in the car wasn't exactly what the doctor ordered for a woman who was due to deliver a baby in another week. That must be the answer to the backache.

That plus the fact that she'd insisted on cooking her own family a Christmas dinner that same evening, complete with stuffed bird, cranberry sauce, pumpkin pie and all the cookies she and the kids had been baking for weeks. By the time she'd served it, she'd found her own appetite was nonexistent.

Lovingly she massaged her enormous tummy, trying to relax the taut muscles. She'd never have believed a woman's skin could stretch so far until she'd experienced it herself.

Tom glanced up from the train set and surprised her in mid-wince. The warmth and love shining from his emerald eyes changed instantly to a look of concern. With a murmured word to Jeb, he got to his feet and came over to kneel beside her chair.

"How are you feeling, Mama?" Gently he splayed a big hand over her swollen belly. "In a couple of weeks, after Master Damien makes his appearance, this will seem amusing."

They'd known for several months now that their first baby, conceived during the earliest days of their marriage, would be a son. Anticipation fizzed like sparkling wine through Tannis's system. She could hardly wait to hold Tom's baby, to put it to her breast for the very first time.

Her face softened with love as she caressed his lean cheek with her fingertips. "I'm okay. I don't mind. I know it'll all be worth it—oh!"

The pain was a little sharper than the previous dull twinges. It had a definite beginning and an equally definite end.

Tom's hand still rested on the mound of his child. "That was a contraction! I felt it!"

"I don't think so. I just overdid it today," Tannis responded. "My back is killing me, but I'll be fine tomorrow."

Tom laughed. "Honey, you'll be more than fine tomorrow, you'll be a mother. You forget I've done this twice before and I know a real contraction when I see one. Did it hurt?"

"Well, yes, a little, but—"

"See? If it wasn't real labor, you wouldn't have felt pain. Have you been feeling mild cramps for a while?"

Excitement began to edge in around Tannis's composure. "Since shortly before dinner. I just thought the drive was too much."

Tom grinned in satisfaction. Gathering Tannis into his arms, he gave her a thorough kiss. "I'm going to call the doctor and tell him we'll be needing his services tonight."

"What?" Amy's book thudded to the coffee table, and she leaped to her feet. "Is Tannis having the baby?"

"Not right this minute, but yes, your new brother will probably be here by tomorrow."

"Holy cow!" Amy rushed from the room. "I'd better get to work on that baby afghan I started crocheting."

"All-l-l right!" Jeb jumped up, too. "I can carry her suitcase. I'll bring it downstairs."

"Thanks, son." Tom clapped him on the shoulder as Jeb bolted from the room.

"What a pair. They're as thrilled about this baby as we are." He turned amused green eyes back to her. "Now are you sure you want to go to the hospital for this? A home birth could be an exciting event."

She shot him a narrow glare. "I know you've lost your phobia about illnesses, but that's going overboard." Then her face softened as she shared his humor. Since the day they'd had their first, and last "Big Fight," as Jeb had referred to it, Tom had showered her with more love than she'd ever expected to know.

Another contraction hit and she breathed, aware of him timing her. He continued to monitor her through several more contractions, finally catching her gaze with his own again. "These are only three minutes apart. Even though they aren't bad yet, we'd better get ready to go."

"They aren't bad yet?" She rolled her eyes. "Says who? Why didn't anyone tell me how this felt? I think I want to cancel this performance and just wait for the stork to drop a package down the chimney."

Tom leaned forward again to press a possessive kiss onto her lips. "Sorry, honey, you can't opt out now." He caressed the mound where his child rested. "I'm glad the big moment is at hand. I'm anxious to hold my child, but I'm just as anxious to hold you in my arms again. I've missed you, Mrs. Hayes."

She smiled at his euphemistic language. Their love-making had been suspended three weeks before on doctor's orders. "I've missed you, too. And there's something else I've missed."

"What's that?" He didn't sound pleased that she'd found something else she couldn't do without.

Tannis smiled, a secret smile just for him. "Our hot tub trysts. It'll be nice to—"

Another contraction, a bit stronger than the last, sneaked up on her and she found that this time she couldn't talk through it.

"Breathe, honey. Remember what we learned." Tom was concentrating on his watch. He rose to his feet. "Hmmm. Two minutes since the last one. This is moving faster than I expected. I'd better call the doctor and help Jeb with that suitcase." He started to run from the room, then turned back and dropped to his knees beside the rocker.

Splaying both hands over her belly, he gazed into her eyes with the intensity she'd loved from the very beginning. "I love you, Tannis. Thank you for not giving up on me."

She laid her hands over his, loving the feel of his big hands on her body. "I feel so lucky. To have found you…and to share our love. I wasn't about to give up on you. Because that would have meant giving up on *us*. I knew it was time for you to move on, to love again. It was time for me."

"Time for Tannis." He smiled, then rose to his feet as she panted through another contraction, helping her up as soon as it was over. "And time for our last Christmas present. Let's go welcome our son into the world."

*   *   *   *   *

Take 4 bestselling love stories FREE

Plus get a FREE surprise gift!

Rugged and lean...and the best-looking,
sweetest-talking men to be found in the
entire Lone Star state!

Diana Palmer

LONG, TALL TEXANS

In July 1994, Silhouette is very proud to bring you
Diana Palmer's first three LONG, TALL TEXANS.
CALHOUN, JUSTIN and TYLER—the three cowboys
who started the legend. Now they're back by popular
demand in one classic volume—and they're ready to
lasso your heart! Beautifully repackaged for this
special event, this collection is sure to be a
longtime keepsake!

"Diana Palmer makes a reader want to find a Texan
of her own to love!" —*Affaire de Coeur*

**LONG, TALL TEXANS—the first three—
reunited in this special roundup!**

**Available in July,
wherever Silhouette books are sold.**

Silhouette®

LTT

SILHOUETTE® Desire®

Big Bad WOLFE

WOLFE WATCHING
by Joan Hohl

Undercover cop Eric Wolfe knew *everything* about divorcée
Tina Kranas, from her bra size to her bedtime—without ever
having spent the night with her! The lady was a suspect, and
Eric had to keep a close eye on her. But since his binoculars
were getting all steamed up from watching her, Eric knew it
was time to start wooing her....

WOLFE WATCHING, Book 2 of Joan Hohl's devilishly sexy
Big Bad Wolfe series, is coming your way in July...only
from Silhouette Desire.

It's our 1000th Silhouette Romance, and we're celebrating!

Join us for a special collection of love stories by authors you've loved for years, and new favorites you've just discovered. Join the celebration...

April
REGAN'S PRIDE by Diana Palmer
MARRY ME AGAIN by Suzanne Carey

May
THE BEST IS YET TO BE by Tracy Sinclair
CAUTION: BABY AHEAD by Marie Ferrarella

June
THE BACHELOR PRINCE by Debbie Macomber
A ROGUE'S HEART by Laurie Paige

July
IMPROMPTU BRIDE by Annette Broadrick
THE FORGOTTEN HUSBAND by Elizabeth August

SILHOUETTE ROMANCE...VIBRANT, FUN AND EMOTIONALLY RICH! TAKE ANOTHER LOOK AT US! AND AS PART OF THE CELEBRATION, READERS CAN RECEIVE A FREE GIFT!

YOU'LL FALL IN LOVE ALL OVER
AGAIN WITH
SILHOUETTE ROMANCE!

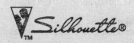

CEL1000

Coming in June from

SILHOUETTE® Desire®

BEWILDERED
by Jennifer Greene
The latest in her
spellbinding series

The sexy, single Connor brothers are each about to
meet their perfect partners—with lots of help from a
matchmaking pirate ghost named Jock.

In June, get to know Michael, a man who believes romance
is for fools—till he meets his own true love.

"A spellbinding storyteller of uncommon brilliance, the
fabulous JENNIFER GREENE is one of the romance
genre's gifts to the world of popular fiction."

—Melinda Helfer, *Romantic Times*

SILHOUETTE® Desire®

They're sexy, they're determined, they're trouble with a capital T!

Meet six of the steamiest, most stubborn heroes you'd ever want to know, and learn *everything* about them....

August's *Man of the Month,* Quinn Donovan, in
FUSION by Cait London

Mr. Bad Timing, Dan Kingman, in
DREAMS AND SCHEMES by Merline Lovelace

Mr. Marriage-phobic, Connor Devlin, in
WHAT ARE FRIENDS FOR? by Naomi Horton

Mr. Sensible, Lucas McCall, in **HOT PROPERTY**
by Rita Rainville

Mr. Know-it-all, Thomas Kane, in **NIGHTFIRE**
by Barbara McCauley

Mr. Macho, Jake Powers, in **LOVE POWER**
by Susan Carroll

Look for them on the covers so you can see just how handsome and irresistible they are!

Coming in August only from Silhouette Desire!   CENTER